A TRICK I
LEARNED FROM
DEAD MEN

Kitty Aldridge

WINDSOR
PARAGON

First published 2012
by Jonathan Cape
This Large Print edition published 2012
by AudioGO Ltd
by arrangement with
The Random House Group Ltd

Hardcover   ISBN: 978 1 4713 1296 0
Softcover   ISBN: 978 1 4713 1297 7

British Library Cataloguing in Publication Data available

Printed and bound in Great Britain by
MPG Books Group Limited

For Esther

It's not that I'm afraid to die. I just don't want to be there when it happens.

Woody Allen

For dust thou art, and unto dust shalt thou return.

Genesis 3:19

So it goes.

Kurt Vonnegut

PROLOGUE

Never saw it coming. Not in a million. You don't. The story fattened up in the retelling. They do. A shame, they said. A pity. It started with her, of course, that was the beginning. Then him that didn't deserve it. Then it was the youngest. Or was it the eldest? Or both? None of us could explain it, not even me. I should know. I am the eldest. Or was. I have forgotten. That is to say I remember but I don't look back. That is to say I look but I don't dwell.

It was talked about. Still is. One of them was deaf or was he blind? Tragic, yes. This is how they talk. Of course, looking back you could see it coming, they say. The hand of fate, the finger of God, or was it the wheel of fortune?

Nice boys, they didn't deserve it: this I have heard at the post office, the pub, Somerfield. And I have heard: They were strange. And also: They were perfectly normal. I've heard it all: They deserved it. It was foretold. And more.

Hard to recognise yourself in the tale they tell. This new folklore turns you and yours inside out till you can't see what was once your own. Out of the mists stroll you, re-drawn. The new you is a fable, a warning. So our lives go. The trouble comes slowly at first. It always does. These things happen. C'est la vie.

1

SOME CLEAR SPELLS IN THE EAST, CLOUDING OVER LATER IN THE EVENING

You knock first before you go in. You don't wait of course.

Good morning, Mr Gillespie. Lee here. Nice day.

Everyone is known by their formal name: Mr, Mrs, Miss. We have not yet had a Lord or Lady, but we had a Doctor and a Major. Babies and kiddies are their first name. Everyone is someone. They have status, the dead. Derek said that. It's true, you're somebody when you're dead, you get respect.

Derek has started on Mr Gillespie, but I must take over, as Derek's off to the crem for a two o'clocker. I pull on latex gloves. Three out today, Mr Gillespie, I say. We've got our skates on, I say. I find a bit of chat breaks the ice. I thread up and open Mr Gillespie's mouth. Here at Shakespeare & Son it matters not what you did when you were alive, we don't look back. What matters is the here and now. Your status as a deceased individual makes you important, a VIP. True to say for some it's a first taste of VIP treatment. Death is an egalitarian state, red carpet all round. All are equal at Shakespeare & Son, no one is better than.

A great leveller, death, Derek says. He tends to talk through his nose. Derek Locklear has been an undertaker for nigh on eighteen years. He fell into it when his establishment, The White Stag, near Junction 4 by the flyover, went bust. You

1

never know what's around the corner, he says. On day one he tells me, Lee, you've got an old head on young shoulders. I took it as a compliment; I'm twenty-five next birthday. Granted he rabbits for England, but Derek is chock-full of wisdoms. A waste really, as most of it falls on deaf ears.

Derek's still got his mutton-chops and waistcoat, but he took to funeral care like a duck to water. Derek is not the boss; Howard Day is our funeral director, he runs the shop. He speaks poshly, which is important when you're dealing with the dead, people expect it, it gives them faith.

Lee Hart is a knob. Someone wrote it on the bus shelter. I know who. Sticks and stones. You have to rise above it. I no longer use the bus service, I walk everywhere, it's better—get out and see the world.

Some people reckon there's not much to funeral care, but there's more to it than meets the eye. I am learning at Derek's elbow, as he's been there and back. I am Derek Locklear's apprentice. Some people call him Del. I didn't expect to wind up in the trade either, funny. I had my eye on Communication Technology, a pipe dream, as it turned out. We all enter these doors in the end, think on. At my age I am what you call the early bird here, but still. Basically it helps to have the right personality, death doesn't suit everybody; lucky I was born for it.

Hang on while I fetch my scissors, Mr Gillespie. Nearly done, I say. I don't see the need to work in silence, it's not a library. Derek has Radio 5 on.

Everything sinks after death, Mr Gillespie has loose folds. Funny how bones rise up as deterioration begins, but it's natural as. Everything

2

dissolves in the end, it's the process. A face shows its skull, a challenge for us. No point dwelling. The trick is be positive, be respectful, even when you're pushed for time. Mr Gillespie has all his own teeth, not a full set, but still.

Here we go, Mr Gillespie, I say. I tilt his jaw and go through the soft palate with my long needle; there is a little pop—same as when we needle-threaded our paper mâché sculptures at school for hang and display—a million years ago seems.

Shakespeare & Son Funeral Services is situated between the old council estate and the playing fields. A pebble-dashed single-storey, you wouldn't look twice. Mind you, when the sky is blue the roof looks red, when it is in fact brown. At the other end of the street is a pub called The Ship. We don't drink there.

I tend not to vary my route. Often you don't see another soul, just the birds calling, sound of your shoes on the lane. Animals raise their heads when they see you. Just me, Lee, I say. Same old. Harvest time you might meet a giant contraption coming the other way. The combine is wider than the road, hung with choppers, spreaders, you name it. You have to step in the ditch for it to pass. Contractors nowadays, strangers in the cab; everyone knew everyone when we were at school. I'm not saying it was better.

Takes a minute to get out of the ditch without making a mess of my trousers. I wear a suit for work. It's a question of respect. I have two suits and I rotate them. I have three self-ironing shirts off eBay. I bought them with a pinch of salt, but they have proved to be worth their weight in gold.

3

On clear mornings you can see the forest from the bridge over the dual carriageway. It sweeps to the left, widens, curves around to the right. I hadn't realised a forest could do that, turn like a river. Not a natural forest of course, but still. Sometimes there is mist on the carriageway. Cars hurtling blind, dangerous. I catch the face of a driver looking up, seeing me, afraid I might jump. Funny. I wave but they're already gone.

My friend, Rob Avon, works at Gatwick Airport. The Red Lion is our local. It is your average pub, a few hundred years old with a resident ghost and subsidence. Rob Avon, aka Raven. The name harks back to his Goth phase—he still dyes his hair black, but he's left the eyeliner behind.

Local ale we do partake of. We sit in the corner beside the grizzly bear; a feat of taxidermy, the landlord calls it, which is fine if you speak good English. The bear was a performer, once upon a time, he still wears the collar and chain. You could feel sorry for him, except that he's roaring his head off, even now he's dead. Not to worry, he won't hurt you.

You don't have to be mad to work here. Someone's crossed out mad and written dead. A stab at humour. It was Derek who brought the word foible to my attention; I try to use it in conversation, without wanting to come over as a ponce. I also find *per se* creeping into my everyday speech. I was wary but so far no one's said, Don't be a knob, Lee, that's French.

Amazing what people take with them. Ancient Egyptians, all of us. You couldn't make it up. They say you can't take it with you; you can. So long as it's

4

not cash. If the family requests it, we do it, within reason, nothing flammable obviously. Personal Effects are the items accompanying the deceased inside the coffin. First time I tucked a cheque for a million between the fingers of one of our gents I thought, nice one. Brilliant, basically. I'd like that for myself. Who doesn't want to die a millionaire? Tax free.

It's the little things, the in-jokes, the ironic touches that lift people's spirits. Death can leave a person's sense of humour intact, it's not all doom and gloom.

Any coffin details for these?

On the side, right in front of you. Mr Keegan's done. Other two need doing. Is that kettle on?

Mr Keegan is going to wear his own clothes. Winchester coffin. White lining. No crucifix. Personal Effects: Panama Slim Panatellas 6 Pack. Omega watch, initials engraved. Letters. Photograph of a smiling woman. Everything must be recorded in the big book. Everything is written down.

Mr Tomlinson is wearing his own clothes, to include a PJ Brown construction helmet. Embalm yes. Viewing to be arranged (TBA) but yes. Cremation. He will lose his hat in that case. Health & Safety v. Health & Safety, ironic. But not as ironic as the cremation of the fireman last year. Death is full of irony.

Mrs Ferguson: Oyster gown. Oyster frill. The Ripon. Embalm no. Ashes Casket: Standard.

5

Personal Effects: Musical box. Photograph of canal boat. Packet of Bird's Custard Powder. Viewings: TBA. Jewellery: TBA. I wonder if the boat was owned or rented. I've never tried Bird's custard.

Mr Muldarney is causing a stir. The Basic Coffin. Blue frill. Gown. Embalm no. Viewing: TBA. Awaiting crem details. Personal Effects: A photograph of a little boy, smiling. Set of teeth. An onion.

Yours truly despatched to Somerfield for said onion. If you don't laugh, you'll cry. I said that to Derek. I produced the onion from behind my back. He said, Don't piss about, Lee, there's three still to do.

Nil effects it says on Mrs Parkinson's column. Derek puts her in the basic pink and matching coffin frill. No viewings. Derek brushes her hair out of respect, but he doesn't fetch his make-up box. I check her sheet and tuck it under her plate. All done and dusted.

Two funerals out. Four in their boxes. Three out tomorrow, two Thursday, two Friday; busy but not murder. Five out is madness, happens now and then, total insanity. Getting from one to the next, it'll turn your hair grey, it did Mikey driving the hearse, fact. You can't put your foot down.

*   *   *

We live in the end cottage on Cinders Lane, where it meets Lye's Cross. Our mum remarried: Lester has been ill of late. He is on medication. He has to

6

write down his dosages, or else he gets muddled. He had to take early redundancy from his work at Dinnages. Downhill ever since, worse after she died. Our real dad is a plant operator; currently we are not sure exactly of his whereabouts.

As I raise my door key, I catch sight of my brother, Ned, stepping out of his bedroom window on the first floor. Ned is not everyone's cup of tea. I hear the twang of springs. Ned appears over the hedge in mid-air, frog legs, then drops out of sight again. Twang. I let myself in. I am the eldest.

She used to say, Lee, if you can't love your own blood, then who?

We got the trampoline second hand: an Emperor twelve-footer (no safety net), thirty-nine pounds off eBay.

I put the tea on, sausages. I boil water for spuds. I open a tin of peas.

Cup of tea would be nice if you're making, Lester shouts at the TV. I've only got one pair of hands, I say. I put the kettle on. *Extreme Makeover*, he watches it around the clock. She would've switched it off. Different since she died.

Ned seems to step out of the wall, gives me a jolt.

Fuck! Fright you me, I sign him. He laughs.

My brother was not born deaf. His deafness arrived in disguise when he was four months old. His deafness is my fault, this has been proved. I don't dwell because you can't turn back time.

Ned looks at the steam coming off the spuds, hair in his eyes, sweat on his nose.

Gravy? Gravy? he signs.

Patience, I sign back. Bollocks, I think to myself.

He is breathing through his open mouth, air whistling through the gap in his teeth, his long bare

7

toes are splayed, his back slightly curved. In the old days I used to imagine him with a tail. He spins out, slamming the door. Ned's got a temper, always did. She used to say he got it off the elves. Whatever.

You wouldn't think we were brothers. Ned has a mole below his lip, like a girl, his hair belongs to our mother, thick, shiny; if it wasn't for his stubbly Adam's apple you might be fooled. I have someone else's hair entirely, frizzy, our dad's probably. If I knew his whereabouts I would complain. I have no moles or free gifts from nature. I have thin legs and high eyebrows, like I don't know what the hell's going on. I have a long back which Lester says will turn against me in later life; he takes co-codamol for his.

We learned to sign together, she taught us. Ned's hands are two birds: tap, bounce, glide. My hands are slow, even now. His hands can tell you any story, plus exaggerations, in seconds. The beads on his wrist make a noise like rain: it is the sound of Ned, like a human black cloud pouring down. He will never know.

I have a photo of her: me and Ned under each arm, two chicks, she called us. Back then I used to put our old washing line in his mouth and whip him with a birch. We were ten and eight. This was our carriage, Ned was the horse. I steered by pulling left or right. If he disobeyed he got a tap, if he was slow he got a tap. We went all over, lanes, fields, woods. He never whinnied and no one saw our carriage because it was invisible. I don't ask him if he remembers it.

He was a gifted child. She told me that. I believed her. She was terrified he might wander on to the dual carriageway: Ned was drawn to electric fences, lightning, canals, traffic. I thought about that. I told him deaf people couldn't die. I thought it would cheer him up. I led him to the dual carriageway. Not to hurt him, on the contrary, I wanted to watch him survive, use his gift, see how he did it. A gap in the traffic, off he ran, arms out like a bird. No fear. Halfway across he stood at the crash barrier, waving, watching the cars rocketing. The horror on the drivers' faces made us laugh, the brake lights flashing as the cars slowed. Result! I was proud, the effect he had, definitely a gift. What a laugh. I waved. He waved. And when he sprints back, the blare of horns. Magic. We scarper before someone calls the police, change our clothes so we won't match any description.

We screamed, it was blinding. We were Samurai.

Where our garden ends by the barbed wire the field starts. Crop in there, oilseed rape. Clackety-clack it goes in the wind, like applause in a giant stadium. Good evening, Wembley. I take a bow. Split the pods with your thumbnail and black seeds fall out. A knob comes on a tractor and does it. I watch him smoking his fags, taking his breaks, staring at his mobile phone. He's got a big red ear that doesn't match the other. Who'd text him? His sister probably. Dead romantic. The phone mast is on the west side. One of them with sponge fingers. They give you cancer apparently. Not sponge fingers, phone masts. Maybe sponge fingers do too, I wouldn't like to say.

On the east side ridge is oak and elm in a line like they're waiting. Everything waits. Crows sleep there at night, fifty million judging by the sound.

9

From her bed she watched this field: the weather, the mechanical sprayer, the red-eared knob. She liked it. We put her ashes there. We waited till the wind dropped, around March time.

This morning from the landing window I catch sight of Ned running in the field along the set-aside. He is wearing flip-flops. I watch. He stumbles, runs on. Must have seen a hare or something, he likes hares. He won't get close flapping about like that: unaware of the noise he makes. I try to imagine what someone not related to him would think. I know what I'd think. I don't know how he got this way. I try to rewind in my mind but I just go around in circles.

I used to carry him on my back. He liked it, bit of a laugh. Started when he was a nestling and I was six or seven. We still do it on a special occasion. Dog, he called me when he was learning to sign the alphabet, but he got it wrong. Gog, I was instead. Gog I remain to this day. He signs it as a shape now, a finger drawn across one eye, like I'm half-blind, when in fact I see everything, clear as. One of his foibles.

The JobCentre have Ned's details. He's hoping for BSL interpreter work. He could teach but he won't do the exam. Problem is he won't travel any distance on his own. He lip-reads fine, but. People shout, make like he's stupid. More than likely he's lost his self esteem. Les will look for work once his health is on track. Plan is to sell the cottage. Get solvent. Get a flat nearer town. *It is for the best*. This is our motto. We should have it over the door, we should have it strung in fairy lights at Christmas. I

10

aim at Ned, a single head shot with my bare hands.
Down he do go.

WINDY, BUT WITH HAZY SUNSHINE DEVELOPING FOR MOST, WITH OCCASIONAL HILL-FOG

For my next trick I shall make a dead man walk. No drum roll, please. Is that kettle on? Derek has a box of make-up, a box of tricks, he calls it. He opens a palette of eyeshadows and brushes.

There are two chilled rooms, chapels, we call them. Relatives can view their loved ones in an open coffin. We don't embalm, we don't have the facilities or the space or an embalmer. If it's required they go to Redhill to be embalmed, a day trip. We are a small outfit.

Derek begins. He talks as he works.

It's a question of light and shade, Lee. Rembrandt was the master. It's the subtle touches, shade here, dab there, a client should look their best. This is a big day for them, big as their birthday.

Derek brushes Peach Flush over Mrs McKinnon's cheeks and brow. He cocks an eye in my direction. It's a talent, he says, but don't be intimidated by that. Technique is the byword. We tender a service, that's all.

Derek blows the excess powder off Mrs McKinnon, steps back, narrows his eyes at me. It's not for us to have an opinion, Lee. The fewer opinions you have, the better you'll get along, son; the dead don't care what you think.

Using a wider brush, he adds a dusting of Sunset Tropic. He opts for cocoa eyeshadow, blending it with a paler shade. He picks Hot Sensation for the lips.

In my opinion Derek overdoes the make-up. I'm not talking about the men but these ladies are ringing alarm bells for me. Unsubtle is the word. Only one relative has remarked thus far, but. Then again he works miracles with disguise, when it's required. You can't have your cake and eat it. In his defence Derek says, No woman wants to meet her Maker without her lipstick on, fact. Personally, I reckon that's out of date. Then again most of our clients are Derek's era and beyond. It's not my place to say anything, I'm only the trainee.

Howard Day has a hurried step. He takes pride in his appearance, smart in his suit. He has his hair cut twice a month, buffs his nails. He is a fan of the Tour de France.

He has a special, hushed voice for relatives.

Do please take a seat. Sit yourself down. Can I get anyone anything? Tea? Coffee? Milk? Sugar? Sure?

A soothing voice. You could nod off. Not to be funny but Howard has the touch with the relatives, the full package: patience, interest, concern.

Take your time, he says. Would you like me to run through things again with you?

He keeps his knees together, his head on one side, his voice soft. I'm making it sound easy, it's not. He knows what to say and when to say it. He could've been a vicar, no problem, could've done it with his eyes closed.

Shall we take a little breather for five minutes? he says. Is there anything else I can help you with? He leaves a gap after he speaks. Putty in his hands, the families are. His Achilles heel is personal property. No one is allowed to touch the silver-topped cane he uses when he steps out in his topper to lead the coffins. His broomstick, Derek calls it.

Outside I can hear Mikey whistling. He calls his hearses by name, created from their registration plates. Now, now, children, he says to them. They just stand there in the garage.

That's you lying there stark bollock, Derek says. It's always you, Lee, because one day it will be. Pure Derek, that one. A Derekism in fact.

They look asleep after Del and me have done our secret tinkering. I say secret because it is. There is no Magic Circle per se, no pledge, but still. You don't talk about it, truth be told. It's a secret you have with the deceased, a pact.

Saying that, there is a peacefulness to this job. You come at the end, after the fact. I'm not cut out for illness, suffering. I prefer to step in when that's done. People say to me, What's it like then, a dead body? I always hesitate, but if I were forced to describe it, at gunpoint so to speak, a dead person is like a newborn, weird, other-worldly, but. Familiar as your own face in the mirror.

I bring in the post for Irene. She mans the office phones. Irene has a sympathetic voice which, even so, manages to make you feel you have let her down in one area. A lot of women have this talent, but Reen has honed it to perfection. She says she was born with a good phone voice, now she uses it to chase up unpaid bills; hers is the first and last voice relatives hear at Shakespeare's. She extracts

14

large sums off the grief-stricken. A dirty job but. Someone's got to. A youngster couldn't do it, you need someone with a bit of experience, like Irene. Behind her back it has been mentioned that Reen could get a PIN number off a dead man. I've witnessed her performing her phone voice while picking the radicchio out of her chicken ciabatta and still achieving a positive result. You can't teach that. Respect, Reen.

*   *   *

Derek says I can leave early, so me and Ned go to Casteye Wood. I take my .22 air rifle. I added a scope and mounts last year. I get the odd pigeon now and then. Ned doesn't like pigeon meat. When I hit one he cradles the thing home in his arms, its head lolling. When it comes to animals, he speaks their language. He lost his job at the kennels when they closed it down. I tell him I'll help him get another job, but he won't have it.

We both frequent these woods, though I consider myself more of a regular. The air is green in here. We stumble on the tree roots, quite a laugh, seriously mental underfoot. I push him and he pushes me back. Ned has a laugh that puts people in mind of giant elves: deep, but with a hint of Disney. We share a smoke, take our time, think on. These beech are two hundred years old, they grow like webs. Ned gawps up at the canopies, mouth open, arms spread. I could aim but of course I don't.

*   *   *

Lester is in his chair. Same story since he was made redundant. Lost her, lost his job, lost the will. Once upon a time he sang 'Born to Run' in his swimming trunks while constructing an alpine rockery in the back garden as a birthday gift for her.

Same old on TV: first they destroy someone's home, then they build them a new one for free. Someone shouts, *Would you like to see inside your house?*

I take the weight of the .22 on my arm and stare ahead at the bald patch on the back of Lester's head. A TV reality woman covers her mouth with both hands. No one would ever know. Not even Les. I picture his brains on the rug. Only joking, but still. A pigeon is one thing. No way could I harm a human. Wrong weapon anyhow.

Tesco Mince & Onion Pie it says on the box. I pop it in at one eighty.

You hungry? I call. Nothing.

In the old days we watched TV together, nowadays Lester has assumed sole control of the remote. Seen one *Extreme Makeover*, seen them all, I leave him to it. When Ned lost his job I let him have the MacBook upstairs in his room. Mistake. That leaves me with the microwave and the kettle. Whatever. I usually have a can in the kitchen, a Stella, relax in the chair. I listen to the radio. Not just music. Last month they had a funeral director. Game on! Runs his own business in America. He wrote a book on it. Everything he said, it could have been me. I put my fist in the air. Fame at last. Nice one. I rang Derek. We're on the radio, I said. Guess what? Americans say casket instead of coffin. I rang Mikey. Guess what, Mike? I rang Howard. Please only use this number for work, Howard said.

16

Then he said he would listen to the programme, definitely. Thanks for the tip, he says.

I have given up asking Les if I can watch something on telly. He won't speak a whole sentence, just the odd word like, No.

Dial.a.TV offer a 28-inch Widescreen for £4.84 a month. As a rule I avoid Direct Debit but. This time next week I could be watching *I'm a Celebrity Get Me Out of Here*.

*   *   *

Crows don't like the woods, they leave it to the pigeons. One there now, blowing out the same old notes. My mate, Raven, says the wood pigeon's song is the *Close Encounters* theme backwards. I keep meaning to test it, but my schedule's pretty full. You can see the lane through the trees from here.

An incident took place last month, people are still talking about it. One of the farm workers frightened a girl, chased her down the lane. I'd put my money on the red-eared knob if I were a betting man. Reckon it was likely him. Policeman came a-tapping. Did we know? Did we see? Description is of a blonde man, possibly of Nordic origin. Sorry, I said, we knew nothing about it.

Ned stood behind me reading the policeman's lip talk, shaking his head. No, no. Neither of us know anything at all. Sorry about that. Then I mentioned the red-eared knob. You might want to talk to him, I says. Something about him, I can't put my finger on it.

Is he blond, they ask.

More or less, I say.

Thank you, they say. They would look into it.

Cheers, I say. No problem.

You can't be too careful. The girl is eighteen, I heard. She's got three A levels. Fortunately she ran to Rowntree Road and hailed a passing car. If she'd gone the other way, she would have run into fields. Different story then.

Funny thing is she ran right past our door. We might have seen her had we been in. I might have seen her running towards our house, frightened. She might have beat her fists on our door. I could have let her in, reassured her, phoned the police, settled her down. Never fear, Lee is here. But she ran past our house. She headed for a busier road, looking for motorists. Pity. I would have helped. I would have sorted it for her, no problem.

Mrs Carmichael is light as a feather in my arms. I have a problem with hospital sticky tape, as it leaves a grey mark. We have the greatest regard for our friends in the medical profession but they tend to act on the spur of the moment, needs must, but still. Sticky tape and bruising for ever.

What's done is done, Mrs Carmichael. The worst over now.

Just because a person is dead I don't see any point dwelling on the dark side. Here is a woman bid arrivederci to pain, sadness, discomfort, whathaveyou. Her suffering is done. Free as a bird, aren't we Mrs Carmichael? I don't blame the medical profession, they have a job to do, same as, but. As far as they are concerned life is everything, end of. The difference is they don't rate you once you're dead and we do. I'm just saying. It all boils down to this: they believe life is sacred, we believe

18

death is too.

I go up the road lunchtime. Crow sits on the telegraph pole by the old post office. He waits there like a chess piece. Crow thinks he's an eagle, you would at those heights. He steps off casual, skateboarding, wheels, lands on a No Parking sign. When the sun hits him, he goes like a mirror, even his eyes.

I like the Healthy Living Salads from Tesco, though the dressing stains my trousers. In the afternoon the lovely Lorelle drops off the sympathy blooms from Fleurtations. I toss away my yoghurt and hurry out when I see the van.

Hey, I say.

Hey, Lee, she says. All right?

Lorelle: One of life's optimists, always smiling. Possibly from working with flowers or she could've just been born like it. Happy as Larry, Derek calls her. Lorelle experiences the peaks and troughs of life, whereas here we're a lot more skewed being that we are merely death death death twenty-four seven.

It's not just her happy-go-luckiness, I like the gap between her front teeth, the freckle under her right eye, the way her brown eyes slant down. She has a piece of hair that collapses now and then over her face. She tucks it behind her ear. I put my hands in my pockets to stop me tucking it for her and getting done for harassment.

The phrase, dazzling smile, was made for Lorelle. Talk about knock you down, her smile could send you through a hedge. From her perspective life looks like one mad raving bender of birth, baptism,

19

marriage, death. All the big dates in a human life. P'raps her view is as skewed as mine after all. Nice to have things in common. Saying that, we don't just natter about work. If I bring a brew from the office we discuss varied topics. Or sometimes we just stand with our tea, thinking on.

She has no flaws as far as I can tell other than when she parks the van she mounts the kerb but, I think to myself, So what? She could have her pick of men so I'm not taking anything for granted. I haven't asked her out yet. I don't want to frighten her off. Nice and easy. Tiptoe through the tulips.

What d'you call that? Derek is referring to Mrs Whitmarsh. I have finished Mrs Whitmarsh and reckoned her to look good for someone who is dead.

She looks grey, says Derek. She looks ill, son. Get some colour on her before the resus team arrive.

Despite Derek's superiority I do not take this lying down.

I was going for a natural look, I say.

Well, you've overdone it. She looks terrible, he says. Dear God. No one wants to see their relative looking dead, Lee. They want to see the face they loved back when, OK? An approximation of the good old days, Christmas morning after a nip of sherry. That's the look you're after, he says. Are you with me?

Yes, I say.

Derek smooths back his hair, fastens his waistcoat, turns on the tap to wash his hands. No good them going out looking worse than when they came in, he says. Get some sherry down her, glad

20

tidings to all men, get some peace on earth. And get a move on.

Of all Derek's foibles, having the last word, to my mind, is the most grating.

*   *   *

I like to walk the long way. Blow the cobwebs. I forget about them afterwards, I don't take my work home. I like the wind pushing down Bursthill Lane from Cinder Hill, blows their old selves off me. Wind takes them, the deceased clients, off they go. I get the taste of the woods in my mouth and my legs know where to roam.

Welcome to Our Historic Village, it says on the sign.

OK, cheers!

There is a bird by the public footpath who whistles like a human, every day the same, like he's doing someone's windows with a bucket of suds. No sight of him, but still. I know he's there.

Buonasera, I say. He stops whistling for a moment.

I look for Crow. He waits on the telegraph wire by the postbox. He tilts his shiny eye.

Late again, Lee. You'll be late for your own funeral.

Such wit from a carrion bird.

You got nothing to crow about, I say.

That round goes to me, I reckon. Laters, Mr Corvid.

*   *   *

I always slam the door when I come in. I could just

say, Hello, but only one of them would hear and neither would reply. I could say, I'm home! But what would it achieve?

First thing I see is the dirty dish stack, frying pan on top, upturned like a sombrero. Buenos dias.

The best view in the house is from the sink. I wash the dishes, watch the sun drop into the woods, pyrotechnics. The house makes a giant shadow of itself on the lane. I hang the tea towel on the cupboard door.

Lester has a beard. A result of his TV marathon. He has watched TV non-stop since she died. If you measured his beard you could p'raps even get the date she passed. Possible Les has broken a round-the-clock TV-watching record and none of us know it.

Reality TV is Lester's reality. He won't watch a quiz, game show or drama. The only good news is no news, he says.

What d'you want for dinner, baked potato or omelette?

No answer. Lately he doesn't reply. Gets on my nerves. Deaf is a political party in this house. Lester is tired of news since receiving the worst news he could have imagined. His plan now is to receive no news whatsoever, not even TV or radio. Easy to knock it, but. Seems to work for him. Just the job, as he would have once said.

I do omelette. I add peas and mushroom. Les has his with the reality people. Ned and me have ours with each other. Ned stirs his tea on and on, ting-a-ling. Jesus. Does your head.

I sign him.

Stop tinging fuck!

He burps. I love my family but. Ned will push

you to the edge and pick his nose while you fall off. He has always got away with murder, it's his middle name, whereas mine seems to be *You couldn't do those dishes could you, Lee?*

Legend has it Ned learned to lip-read overnight. He started signing aged three and a half. Made his own signs, redesigned it like he owned it. He's got shapes no one's heard of. He always had a big head. Ned would be a genius in any language. She said that. Fair play to him, but. He still can't iron his clothes. Or get a job. His dream is to be a landscape gardener. Fat chance, as Les pointed out before he gave up pointing things out, There aren't any landscapes left.

OK, there is a certain Je ne sais quoi to Ned. I can see why she thought he was beamed here by some supernatural force: his laughing elves, his flying hands, his noting of things no one else can clock. And OK, he's not a bad bloke, I can see his plus points. We have the odd laugh, granted, and no way does anyone lay a finger on him while I'm around, but. The world and him is a private party, only one VIP. Ned is king in the silent land. I don't begrudge him, I'm just saying. If I had been the supernatural one would she have preferred me? I don't dwell. No point. I am no fool. She'd have gone anyway.

Lee and I have an understanding, she used to say. Lee is my soldier.

I take care of things. I took it as a compliment.

CLOUD AT FIRST BUT DRIER AND BRIGHTER
CONDITIONS DEVELOPING THROUGHOUT THE DAY

You have to tick everything off, make sure they have everything. You wait till their clothes arrive before you prepare them. Once their clothes arrive they're on their way, as if it's a journey, which it is. Gown is easier, done in no time. No need to manoeuvre the client, two flared sleeves and a long bib, clever, you'd never guess that's all there is to it. Whereas your self-clothed client you often have to alter garments to get them on, snip snip. You don't want to drag the skin, especially the oldies, you don't want skin-slip.

Waiting for the clothes can hold you up. Derek says they never had these troubles at the Royal Opera House. That could either be a joke or p'raps he used to work there before he had The White Stag. Ever the dark horse, I'll probably never know. That's how we found out Howard wanted to be a pole vaulter, a chance remark. When I told Derek, he said, Gordon effing Bennett. We all looked at Howard different after that. I'm going to ask him why he dropped pole vaulting and entered undertaking. I'll choose my moment. People are never what you think. Till they're dead, that is.

At Rest. The engraver makes light work of it. Gravograph is a nifty machine, you begin to think of all kinds of things you could engrave. Only drawback is the noise, like a drill through metal, which is what it is. *At Rest* is my preference. *Rest in Peace* is longwinded compared. Derek veers between the two, Depending on my mood, he says.

There are motifs: the men get the swirl, women get roses. Babies have *Asleep*. I haven't had a baby yet, one to dread. I have a few work firsts left to come: newborn, immolation, suicide. All in good time, ready or not.

Everyone dreads a baby. Fortunately they are few and far between. Derek says he can count them on two hands, which is good. Still, you can't shirk if one comes in. Derek does them asleep, sheet folded under their chin. Small children are prepared in a flash. No death mask for them, the skin is plumper, tricking you, making it harder to take. The eye sockets alone let you know they are gone. Children are buried with their freckles fresh on their face. Christening dresses are popular, undone is easier; we've had Buzz Lightyear, skinny jeans. We never say no. Philip Cuell died of spina bifida and took his light sabre with him. Soft toys, iPods, juice. The parents' request is our command. We don't answer the phone. The radio goes off. The satins are white.

*　　*　　*

The woods know me these days.

Evening, Lee. Buenos tardes.

I startle a bird snoozing in a tree.

Hello, Mr Pigeon, not expecting me were you? Fear not, I am unarmed.

He clatters away.

So. Irene says to me on Tuesday, Are you happy, Lee? I'm happy when I'm here in these woods. I should have told her that, I didn't.

I said, 'course, Reen. Kind of a question's that!

25

And she says, OK, my love.

Sometimes, a woman can see right through you. Derek wouldn't ask that in a million. He calls women the female of the species. Sums it up: species. Freaks me when she calls me My love. Like we're having it off in one of the hearses.

I wish I could name the birds. I could google them, but it'd take till kingdom come. I wonder what Irene meant. People expect too much. Time to get real, but. Reality is on TV nowadays, while everyone lives in fantasy-land. For example, my girlfriend Karen and I went out for nearly two years before she said, Lee, I can't see where this is going. This was before I got the job at Shakespeare's and I've often thought she might have taken me more seriously if I'd been an undertaker, but still. Water under the bridge.

I look out for Crow. I think on, nothing too clever. My thoughts tangle up with the weather and the hedges and we go along like we're the same thing.

When we were kids I used to push Ned along here in the pram. I had to fold him in from age eight, knees up. He loved it. If he kicked too much I had to smack him. He enjoyed our little jaunts. I used to push him all the way up Furlong Hill and back. Miles, we went. He wanted to swap over. I explained he was the baby, that was the way it was. He accepted it. I pushed him up to the woods the long way. When I got to the footpath I tipped him out. We had a walk together. He loved being out and about, made a change. Then I'd carry him on my back till he got too heavy. He has never blamed me for his being deaf. He has many faults but blame is not one.

The field is shadowed down the east side, brass-coloured in the middle. The light has elongated the trees. No birds. They must have gone to Fellings Farm, they might have been harrowing. Just a dead pigeon. Buongiorno; not looking his best: headless, gutless, wing torn clean off. Something's given him a good old seeing to. The feathers go under the fence and into the field. I wait by the fence, watch the clouds.

A vista, is what Lester called this view when he first saw it, A marvellous vista. Those were the days when he spoke for the hell of it. He could surprise you with his outpourings, quite articulate then. People change, sometimes they disappear right in front of you.

There is wildlife in these parts, you just have to wait for it to turn up. I am not here for the wildlife, per se. I am merely here, waiting for nothing.

I sit by the spot. Not a grave exactly, is it? I sit there anyway. She is here because she's nowhere else. They start to slip away, the dead. You don't notice at first. It gets hard to remember. That's how it begins: you can't remember something you always knew. That's the beginning. They slip away, they have to. Bit by bit you let them go. You think you won't but you do. You hold on at first, you make yourself remember, pull it all back, but they go. That's the way it is.

*　　　*　　　*

In the beginning was the Word, and the Word was with God, and the Word was God. All things were made by Him and without Him was not any thing made that was made. Derek has typed up his own

27

cut-and-paste Bible extracts so that they fit on a sheet of A4.

In Him was life: and the life was the light of men.

It is stuck on the workshop wall with Blu-Tack. All your well-known quotes, top twenty Bible hits. God's indefinite wisdom, Derek calls it.

He keeps meaning to frame it but deceased clients keep arriving and, as Derek says, there's only twenty-four hours in a day.

Saying that, Derek points out, God did the lot in six. What have I got to complain about? He jinks an eyebrow at me.

The brass. Like him and God are the same. Derek Almighty. Talk about getting above yourself.

Derek, I say. Shouldn't that be infinite wisdom?

Derek looks at it again, looks at me.

Says indefinite here, he says.

Reckon that's wrong, I say.

He looks again. I'll change it, he says. He does, there and then, with his pencil. Infinite, indefinite, he says, Splitting hairs, he says. Hardly the point, is it?

He's in a huff now.

Depends, I say.

On what?

If you believe in God, I say.

It's not as if it's written in stone, he says. No one cares if God is infinite or indefinite, people haven't got time to worry about it.

Howard pops his head round the door, ending the argument, giving Derek the final word. Derek'll have the final word after they've screwed down his lid.

Lee? Got a minute?

Think on. I've cocked something up. Yesterday,

28

the day before. The bruise on Mrs Wright's hand. We sit down in Relatives 1, like we're relatives.

How do you feel about paging, Lee?

Howard folds his hands, smiles, drops his head to the side. I look at his overhang of teeth. I pretend to think. I do not know how I feel about paging. I can hear Howard breathing, it puts me off.

OK, I say. Not a problem.

Good, Howard says. He nods. He smiles. Teethfest. More teeth than he needs, by the look.

Excellent stuff, he says.

Not a problem, I say.

I have shaved Mr Martindale, as requested. He looks buff. Old gents look better after a shave, even dead ones. Hair and nails do not continue to grow after death, I can hereby defrock this old wives' tale. Skin shrinkage gives the impression of growth, it's an illusion. Mr Martindale is to have his prayer book in his hand. He'll look just the job.

Gents are coffined wearing wristwatches, ladies in their jewellery, but it all comes off if they are to be cremated. After the viewings, everything off including wedding rings, though our crem allows them, if requested. Gold melts with the deceased. All those I Do's. All those promises. All those Till Death Do Us's. Where they go we knoweth not.

You hear people say how they seem asleep and true there is a restedness, but a dead face will show you its skull, I never saw a sleeping face do that. Everything sinks. What you see in the naked dead is a skeleton draped. Not to say that it's spooky, just different. It's natural as. Nothing to be scared of.

Derek holds up a photo of a lady smiling, raising

29

her drink to the camera.

Hot date? Mike enquires.

Match.com? I say. Joining in.

Show some respect, Derek says. It's Mrs Barry.

Mrs Barry is in the chiller, tray 5. Derek trollies her down and parks her in front of me. Well? he says.

It is a fact that Mrs Barry has aged a bit in the last two decades. The picture supplied by the son must be twenty-odd years old, or more. I don't know what to say.

I take it as a compliment, Derek says, but this is not a beauty salon and neither is it the Shrine of Lourdes, are you with me?

I don't answer. I don't know the Shrine of Lourdes. But I can see Mrs Barry has lost her joie de vivre. We have to assume it's the same woman in the photo, but. Finally I think of a comment.

We've got our work cut out, I say.

Derek rubs his face, blinks. He holds the photo at arm's length, squints.

I am not a miracle worker, Lee, he says. We are men not gods.

I don't agree or disagree. Sometimes Derek sounds like he stole his words out of a film. Then again, he says, she's come to the right place. He winks, tucks the photo into his waistcoat. It's now or never, as the great man sang, he says.

Fancies himself, does Derek. If he did his own burial plate he'd be on the Gravograph all day.

4

A GREY START BUT BRIGHTENING UP IN THE MORNING
WITH SOME PATCHY CLOUD LATER ON

I walk home. Shake off the day's woes. Highways and byways. Flyover, lanes, woods: gives you peace of mind. Let the dead men sleep. Spend all day with the deceased you'll feel alive on your way home, trust me. Not that I'm complaining. I enjoy my job. I am the eyes and ears for those who see and hear nothing. I keep them up to date with weather, goings-on. I let them know the forecast for their funeral. No joke. Wait till it's yours. Will the sun shine? Snow? Gale force winds? Plain old pissing down? We'd all like to know. On the day you return to dust how about a blue sky? Some prefer a belting storm. Point is people like a forecast.

If I was at B&Q I might have won Employee of the Week by now. We don't do Employee of the Week at Shakespeare's. We should. Good scheme. Keeps everyone on their toes. A customer is a customer; service is service, I see no difference because customers are deceased. Splitting hairs, as Derek would say.

Which would you prefer? Old knobby fiddle-sticks at W. D. Brookes Funeral Services on the High Street showing you the best view up his nostrils? Not to mention his other propensities, as yet unproven, but. Or me?

I'd want a friendly face. A good morning Mr Hart, looks like rain, not to worry, dry as a bone in here.

Mental, yes. But then it's you lying there. Who knows what the dead catch hold of? Not me, not you. Not yet.

I'm home! Old habits die hard.

Ned is watching TV in Lester's chair. Lip-reading Sky News. I switch it off.

He throws back his head, blows through his mouth. The deaf are noisy. Ned slurps, chews, smacks his lips. Stands to reason, not his fault. Like a whale shoots air out the top of his head, Ned blasts it out his mouth. Like he has been at great depths when he is, in fact, a shallow person. Funny, because when he's going mental on the trampoline you'd think he wants to go up and never come down. When all he has to do is hold his breath, float off like a hot air balloon. Adios.

I sign him the alternatives for tea. Don't know the sign for risotto. I have become more cosmopolitan in the kitchen. I mouth it. Ri. Sott. O. Ned has a dead face when he reads you, it's the concentration—it's why his smile takes you all the more by surprise. He smiles at things no one smiles at: shadows, vibrations, rain, knives. His face lets you see everything, no holds barred. Naked, you could call it. Most faces have learned to cover up their nakedness. Only little kids and Ned go as they are.

He had a girlfriend once, Janey. She had a cochlear implant. He met her at a BDA Youth Group Night in Reigate. Les drove him there and back; the last deaf event he ever attended, as it turned out. When she ended it, Ned cut himself off. Closed up shop. Kaput.

He thinks about his dinner. I hug him from

32

behind, surprise him. Boo. He pushes me off. Hates it he does, hugs. I wrap my arms around, squeeze him. He kicks and squirms. I wrestle him for a hug. He can't stand it, any kind of touching. I have to chase him, hold him down. I kiss his head. He gives in in the end. I reckon it's good for him. I do it anyway. No harm done.

I often eat standing up if Ned doesn't come down. I do Lester's on a tray. I should run an old people's home, perhaps: Oldbastards.com. Think on. Time to consider my options. In the old days Les used to say please and thank you, now he says, Fetch us the paper, Fetch us a fresh tea. I prefer working with the deceased. They're better-mannered and you get job satisfaction. I could never go back to the land of the living, not now.

Water swishes upstairs and the pipes let off a groan. Five generations of farmers have lived here, all our grandfathers going back. Granted, this cottage needs some work, plumbing and electrics for starters. Over the years the fields were sold off, lot by lot. She sold the last when Ned was born. Her ashes lie in the ground her family tilled for a hundred years but we hold no claim on it now. Somewhere out there with her rest the bones of our great-grandfather, feeding the GM crops.

Just after she was diagnosed we lay together on the settee, her and me. We watched the fire flames—not a real fire, gas, but still. Everyone is relying on you, she says. I know you won't let me down. Her fingers lay in mine. She stroked my hair. No one else was in the house. I think about this sometimes.

Farming is no life for you boys, she used to say. Farming ties you down. Get out there and do your

33

own thing. The world is your oyster, she told us.

Sun is low, gold light spreads behind the hill. Shadows on the field. I take myself out. Crow cries on the boundary, like a human voice realising he's forgotten something. I sit with my back to the fence. Let the day blow by. Crow always turns up in the end, glides in like a dirty thought—patience is a virtue. Vainest bird in Christendom. I spot him at the top of the highest tree.

Good evening, Lee. On your walkabout?

That I am. How-do?

He bides his time. The silver blink once, twice, tells me he is thinking. Slippery customer. We have an understanding. People see Lee Hart, trainee undertaker, they think of death. People see Crow, deliverer of dark omens, they think of death. Reapers me and him both; nice to have something in common.

The field, the house, the pylons; she used to say if she were a painter she'd paint it. She wanted to leave something behind, once she knew she was dying. I wanted to say, You're leaving me and him behind. But I didn't.

I stop by the phone mast.

Buongiorno. How goes it?

Mast is busy getting people get connected. A job to do. Communication technology, excellent choice. This old grey pole has got them all talking. Natter natter natter. Me and mast stand there, silent like old friends.

I would have gone with a hammer to find him, the girl-chaser. As I understand it, no one has been apprehended as of yet. Across the fields towards the woods, I would have gone straight away, before her tears dried; along the east field set-aside, where you can't be seen from the woods. Slip through the electric fence at the broken place. Quick as a flash. If I'd caught up with him, that would have been my day. Tock, tock. Job done. Arrivederci. He won't be bothering anyone again, no more chasing with intent on our lane. No need to thank me, it was no problem. I realise he is unlikely to repeat his behaviour at the exact same location but if he does fancy a walk down memory lane, buenos dias, here I am. I don't see it happening, but then who sees anything coming? Only after the fact when it's too late. That's the trouble, the future stands behind you, waiting to say boo.

I stroll up the woods; same old, but never the same sky, trees, wind. You have to pay attention. You can go through your life half asleep. You may never wake up. You may never realise you were even alive if you're not careful. I am careful.

I walk the same way. Past the stumps by the fence then along a twisty path into the heart of the wood where it gets dark. Me and Ned used to play here. I used to sign him the names of things he should know: squirrel, pigeon, bra, knickers. Mum and me used to walk here, once upon a time. The three of us would watch the sunset through the trees. This earth is a beautiful place, she'd say. Don't waste your lives. We won't, I said. As if. I still collect sticks for kindling, short ones. Dry them in the kitchen, right size for the wood burner.

The last of the sun pulls the trees into thin shadows. Somewhere a fox is barking. Reminds me of our first ever trophy when we were kids. A dead fox flattened on the south-bound fast lane.

A beauty. Ned's mission was to collect. This was then, but it could be yesterday. I gave him his instructions. Speed was critical, I told him. So, trot-trot. Off he goes. Arms out. Hurry up. Look at him, dainty as. Watch me, Gog! he signs. Yes yes, get on with it. Taking his time. Come on. Peels it off the tarmac. Get a move on. For *fucks*. Sort it out. Here he comes. Better late than. Mad dash. Through the gap in the traffic. Took your time! Pleased with himself he was. Draped in his arms was our fox: twisted, innards swinging. Stinking to the highest. Then he wants to take it home. Talk about a few bricks short of a load. We bury it in a ditch by the flyover. Ned drops to his knees to pray, God knows where he saw that.

The sun is nearly gone. The last light turns the trees black. I sit down under the big beech. I wait. I don't know what for.

It's late when I lock up at night. Les watches TV till the early hours. I boil the kettle for Ned's drink. I shouldn't baby him, but. Helps him sleep. It's only Tesco Value Instant, not Cadbury's. Calms him down. From the landing window you can see plenty if the moon's up. Woods, field, lane. The mast is a giant's dagger plunged in. Magic could happen but it never does.

5

RAIN WILL CLEAR IN THE EAST, LEAVING A WARM BRIGHT DAY, IF CHANGEABLE AT TIMES

Five things girls Can't Resist. For this article alone I buy the magazine. I have Lorelle in mind, in a nutshell. Anything that puts me ahead of the competition. Needs must. I am surprised by the five things, frankly. I was reckoning, cars, money, looks, usuals, but no. Number one is Romance. Girls like a romantic guy, it says. Romantic Guy brings her flowers, chocolates, gifts, it says. He gazes into her eyes, tells her she's beautiful, blah blah blah, thank you very much, bish bash bosh, job done. I think about this. I am pretty romantic. Next is Confident Guy. This gent is totally secure and at ease with himself, it says. He gives off an aura of power and control. Tougher one, this, but not beyond the realms of whatever. Then there is artistic guy. Artistic Guy is spontaneous and lives for the moment. He uses his creativity to woo her. Woo her. Can't say with authority if I am artistic or not. Not off the top of my head. I could ask, but who?

Lee?

Makes me jump. It's Derek. I shove the magazine into my holdall. Spring out the door, like I'm busy. I shall think on.

I can't help feeling sorry for Mr Delapoint in Chapel 1. He's got a look on his face like he's in trouble, though it's not his fault. He had a single tooth at the front, the others were fakes. They lifted out on dental plates, like little horseshoes without the luck. His hands rest in his lap. His gold wedding ring shines under the work light. Till death do us. Irene calls him Mr Dela-pwan, like he's Japanese. Says it's the correct pronunciation, French. I go with what's written down. I don't think it's fair, second-guessing. Mr Delapoint can't answer back.

Howard puts his head in. Let me know, he says, when Monsieur Deelapwon is ready, would you, Lee?

Each to his own. Howard has his own perspective on things. That could be from pole vaulting, I don't know. Apologies, Mr Delapoint, we are not what you'd call multilingual here. Lucky all Derek has to do is engrave it.

There's an old lady crying in the foyer. I say foyer, it's just two chairs and some dried ferns, but that's what Howard calls it. I hurry over to her.

Everything OK? I ask. And then I think, Lee, you knob, obviously things are not OK.

Mrs Jenson, Let's have a sit-down next door, shall we? Howard is at her side like he dropped through the ceiling, offering his elbow, speaking the words, showing the way. He guides her gently towards Relatives 1, with its thick carpet, padded settees, boxes of tissues. Lee will make you a lovely cup of tea, he says. We've got some shortbread today. Let's take our time, shall we?

You learn this job as you go. You start at the kettle and work your way towards the funeral director's desk. It doesn't happen overnight.

Mrs Barry is a tad leaky at this stage. I plug where

38

necessary, mouths are the worst offender. Remedy is to get wadding into the throat and raise the head. Once the nose is plugged you're home and dry. I don't know where we'd be without Webril Roll. I tuck a head block under Mrs Barry. There we go. She can relax while I get on.

Your needle must be long and curved like a half-moon otherwise you will go in but never come out. A closed mouth is hygienic and pleasant to look at. Who wants to peer inside a loved one's gapery as you whisper your final goodbye? Calm and collected is the look, a little assistance is required, the dead don't pose. Under the chin we go. Clever part is diving into the nose from the soft palette and back again through the lip so that when you pull the two ends together the mouth closes, like so, a drawstring purse. Lovely. On our way, Mrs Barry. Once you've got a nice relaxed Mona Lisa smile, you're on; I'm quoting there. Eye caps prevent eye drift, we use perforated ones. Eyes and hands are important to the bereaved; it's where they go to, the places that used to communicate, you've got to get it right. Eyes sink, fact, mouths gape, hands flop. We all require a little help to look our best, the dead are no different. These eye caps come clear or flesh-coloured, we use the clear. The perforations stop the eyelid sliding back, grip it in place. The dead are not supposed to stare, sneak a peek. Inwards is where they are looking, like Saints.

What have you got today, something nice? Reen likes to know what everyone's having. Reen herself sticks to Tupperware, as does Howard. Me and Derek prefer to experiment with wraps, baguettes, tortillas. Tesco do a range. Pricey

39

but a treat, a bit cosmopolitan. Cheers you up. Plus you don't have to decide the night before.

Brie and Cranberry.

Sounds nice.

I had that. I prefer Chicken Tikka.

What have you got then?

Ploughman's Wedge.

Is that Healthy Living?

Dunno.

Doubt it.

Open a window, Irene.

Sorry.

That's why I bring Tupperware.

The office doubles as a canteen. The phones go, even at 1 p.m. If Reen's got her mouth full someone else has to pick it up, it's Russian roulette. We only take thirty minutes for lunch as most funerals and cremations are between 2 and 3 p.m. It's the nature of the beast, as Derek puts it.

After lunch I return to my Five Things Girls Can't Resist. Here we go. Romantic, Confident, Artistic. OK, number four is Foreign Guy. Foreign Guy is foreign. Cheers. Ta. I read it anyway. Foreign Guy comes from a faraway country and probably has a cute accent, it says. His social customs and everyday behaviour might be a little quirky. He is uniquely charming, it says. For fucks. Whatever. Not to worry, four out of five's not bad. Number five is Intelligent/Witty Guy. That's two things. You have to be both in one? It says in the article Intelligent/Witty Guy instigates conversations that are intellectually stimulating. He makes her laugh with his clever sense of humour, it says. He is an intellectual athlete, springing from one topic to

40

another with informed ease. He is never boring. I let out a lungful of air. That is the five things girls cannot resist in a guy. I roll up the mag. I feel depressed. I don't know why. Not that I'm zero out of five, obviously I'm not. Just the tone of the thing, like yeah right, mate, sorry but nowhere here do it say: number six, Total Knob Guy.

Right. Stand back. Miracles are us. I can feel the force. Chop chop.

Derrick snaps on his gloves, spreads his arms. You're no sooner sat down than you're off again.

When they stop dying, Derek says, we'll put our feet up, won't we, Lee? Right. No time like the present, he says.

He points a right-hand finger at me, bends his knees.

It's one for the money. Two for the show. Three to get ready and . . .

He points his left-hand finger at me.

I don't know what comes next. I wait, blank.

Come on!

Is it Elvis?

Derek straightens up, drops his pose, irritated. He sighs as he turns to dig inside his instrument box. Too late now. I have been slow on the uptake. Timing and general knowledge: two of my weaknesses. Elvis. If he'd sung 'Love Me Tender' I might possibly have caught on, but. The trouble with Derek is he has a temperamental streak, slightest thing can throw him, rub him up the wrong way. He was psyched in order to transform Mrs Barry, return her to her former glory; I let him down on the starting grid. Elvis Presley, before my time. In death, as in life, nothing's perfect.

41

*   *   *

Lethal! a swift half? No harm done. The Arms waiteth.

Ravester. You read my mind.

I enjoy these evening pints with Raven. I do not even bother to call them halves. Our usual seats. Vacant as per. Rave faces the door and tells me if someone comes in. We always sit the same old. I face the stuffed seven-foot bear and the toilets. Cosy in the corner, old Grizzly roaring over our heads.

Been busy?

Keith always asks that. He has been landlord here nigh on five years, but he always says the same thing.

Pretty busy, I say. Not as bad as this time last year. Run off our feet in the cold snap.

Keith tuts and shakes his head. He always does that.

Gatwick busy? he asks Raven.

Armageddon, he says.

Keith tuts and shakes his head.

You'd think he was flying the planes, I say to Keith.

Keith slides off with his cloth.

Rave necks his beer. A dagger of hair sticks out of his head. He is a proven exaggerator.

I saw a massive bee earlier, Rave says into his glass.

I do not reply. I was thinking we could discuss women and their foibles and my plans re Lorelle but I've changed my mind. In my head I have prepared a slam-dunk combo of Romantic/

42

Confident/Intelligent/Witty and even Foreign guy all in one, just like that. Kerboom. This time next week I should be high-fiving. Livin' la vida loca.

A man comes in rubbing his hands together. We sit up. We watch him. We look away before he speaks to us.

I've got gammon for tea, Rave says.

Raven's mum does all his cooking and washing. I am tempted to point it out. One for the road? he says. He checks his watch. Before the clock tolleth?

It's only twenty past nine, I say, double-checking. Go on then.

The gammon hangs in the air. I careth not. Things wear you down.

We just sit after that. Think on. The gammon floats off into the stratosphere.

*   *   *

I find Lorelle on my mind almost all the time. When I am asleep she has a habit of creeping up behind me, putting her hands over my eyes. Guess who? I'm not one for games, even in dreams. I'm a big boy, a professional in trade. There are codes of conduct. I'm not up for this sort of thing generally, but. Needs must. Just make-believe of course, but still. When a girl like Lorelle kisses you without prior warning, you sit up and pay attention. And that's when she makes her move. Nice one. Gobsmacking. Even when it's all in your head. Not that I'm complaining.

My brain makes it up as it goes along. Game on. The girl from the chemist, for example, climbed in yesterday. Talk about awkward as. Hello, there, she says cheerily. What can I do for you today? Without

43

waiting for an answer she disappears under the covers. She is very precise. Summer plums, six for a pound. Very reasonable. Methodical you could say, probably because she works in a chemist. For a moment I feel peaceful. I can hear the sea. Doesn't last long. The light dims, a chill sets in. I listen to the click of my breathing.

6

MAINLY DRY ACROSS THE SOUTH AND EAST, MILD AND BREEZY NATIONWIDE

I remember things. Not to dwell, but. In the old days me and Ned would sometimes take off, leave Les struggling, rinsing bowls, washing sheets, swearing under his breath. We would take things from the kitchen: the big bottle of Tango, the Sunday biscuits from the cupboard. We would run to the woods to eat. Then maybe run to Ditton Road to the shops, sit outside the newsagent, burp and fart until the woman from the CoinWash told us we were pigs. What a laugh. Give her the finger. Ned loved it. I would do it again behind her back, copy her waddle walk. Right laugh.

Sometimes we bought sandwiches from the motorway services with the pound coins from the kitchen jar. We'd leg it to the tracks. No trains any more. We'd use a brick to smash things, boring after a while. We'd lie down. We'd pretend train after train was flattening us on the tracks, whistles blowing, brakes squealing; we wished ourselves dead over and over, but not for ever. We'd take a stroll in the open air, two ghosts out and about. I'd light up one of Lester's Dunhills, like a proper country gent, while Ned tossed the tomato slices from his BLT into the trees. On the way home we'd chuck stones at the pigeons in the woods to cheer ourselves up.

Ned would be tired by the time we got back. I'd put him in the pram for a sleep, push his knees down under the blanket. I'd park it behind the shed so he wouldn't disturb her. I'd leave him there till dark. He was a good kid in those days; when he was little he was cute as. This changed of course as he grew slowly but surely into a knobhead, but. I remember I stole him sweets and Fanta from the old newsagent at the bottom of the High Street. I'd clean his face after so he wouldn't get in trouble. He'd do anything for me then and I'd do anything for him. I try not to get nostalgic. I used to conduct simple experiments for his own benefit. Simple things. Teach him to react without the aid of audio sound, stand him in good stead. I'd launch missiles for him to avoid. He didn't always avoid them. Now and then he'd run to her, booing like a baby. I meant no harm, I would not harm my own brother. I was preparing him. Life is hard, no second chances. No one prepared me.

He got me back one time only. What the Sunday paper would call a frenzied attack. He planned it. We both had our shirts off for a tan. He did it by the ditch in Lower Field so he could use the giant nettles. Lashed me with such force he laced his own shoulder too, on the backswing. It could have been either of us screaming or both, I couldn't tell.

I got him back on the way home. Two can play. Surprise! No probs. Half a brick I used. Surprising amount of blood.

Mental she went.

What have you done? What have you done?

Keep your hair on. I remember saying that.

She hit me so hard I landed in the road. Ned loves a bit of slapstick. He laid himself down beside me. Two knobs in the gutter. Put his arm across me in case she tried it again. We still laugh about that. A classic. Years later on TV I saw a man in Pakistan whip himself with chains and it made me think of him.

* * *

You can fall into a rhythm in the workshop, I like that. I set the Gravograph and off it goes. *Evelyn Ann Barry*.

You type it in then the robotic arm does the job. You can turn your attention elsewhere, you can leave the building. The Gravograph cuts the name all by itself. Modern technology, it does your head in. I staple the frills in the box. The York, smart. Once the plate is finished you fix it to the correct coffin. Tap tap, on it goes. With the polonia woods, soft woods, the Salisbury for example, Derek pushes the screws in with his thumb. Mike said he should go on *Britain's Got Talent* with that.

Important to get the plate straight, no excuses. The plate is you: name, dates. It is all you are, a name and two dates. Tell it straight. Derek does it in inches. You use the name on the plate as a guide, measurements down and across; double-check. Your life on a plate. I made that up.

Not to be funny but. You get perspective working here, it can't be helped. We're ready for Mrs Barry.

Derek is blowing on his mug of tea.

Mrs Barry ready? I say.

Ready as she'll ever be.

Derek has done her hair with heated rollers. Combed and sprayed in place it doesn't look too bad. She has a rosy glow. The lipstick makes her look like she's ready for a party. I straighten one of

47

the gold earrings. She looks festive; the red dress, the green silk scarf. Her shoes look brand new. Sure enough there's a sticky label on the sole, £59.99.

Merry Christmas, Mrs Barry, I say. It's not Christmas but Mrs Barry doesn't know that.

Want a hand? Derek calls.

I fold the sheet across her on both sides.

I'll manage, I call back.

I wheel the trolley carrying Mrs Barry's coffin level with Mrs Barry. I swing her feet in first. I get hold of both sides of sheet and lift Mrs Barry across and lower her into her coffin. If you get it right the head should drop directly on to the block. You can make adjustments. Not a textbook landing but Mrs Barry is near as dammit. A tweak here, tug there. I check the paperwork. Wedding ring, earrings, pocket prayerbook, photograph of grandchildren. I tuck the prayerbook under her fingers. The grandchildren in the other hand. I check again. Items in the wrong coffin, items gone walkabout equals professional suicide. I add my signature to the paperwork. I pop the lid on. Bob's your uncle, Mrs Barry. Chapel 2 it says here, viewing at four o'clock. Forty minutes start to finish. Most of that was Mrs Barry's hair. Thirty minutes is my tops, you don't want to rush if you can help it.

*   *   *

An Englishman's home is his castle, so sayeth Derek. He lives on the Peabody Estate, an end of terrace. I go to help him manoeuvre his three-piece suite, so he can repaint his front room. I end up staying all day to help tape his windows, prime the

48

walls, shift the rest of the furniture. We stack it in the garden.

You and me, he says. In my estimation we make a good team.

I don't disagree. I am glad. He makes me a ham sandwich and we sit on the settee under the tree and let our conversation wander.

There is an empty mud hole in the front garden, like one of his graves. It used to be a pond, he says. Somebody poisoned his fish, he says. Envy, he reckons. We stand looking at it for a long time. Now he has geckos indoors. They use a lot of electricity, he says.

7

A GREY START FOLLOWED BY CLEAR SPELLS, THEN
COMFORTABLY WARM WITH SOME SUNSHINE

Lorelle is in. I skid on the prep room tiles. Hurrying
is frowned upon here. She has laid out her blooms
and is double-checking the names. I only just make
it.

Phew, I say. Caught you.

All right, Lee? she says.

Not too bad, I say. Nice blooms, I say.

Yeah. From abroad, she says.

Mikey breezes past.

Selhurst Gardens, Selhurst Gardens, he says out
loud. He turns over his shoulder, shouts towards
the office, Why didn't you tell me before then?

No answer.

Might as well talk to the wall, he tells Lorelle.

I take her hand. Bold or what. Number two:
Confident Guy. I lead on. We find ourselves in
the storage room, where it's quiet. No electrics
allowed here due to the cremated remains. No
good the ashes in ashes. We only burn them once.
The poly containers are stacked high against the
glass partition, making the room dim. Each tub is
labelled in permanent marker. **Please label urn and
file alphabetically,** it says on the wall. **Please make
sure cremation certificate goes to office for filing.
Thanks!**

The names climb high above Lorelle's head.
Janine Boyce, it says beside her ear. The remains
are transferred to caskets when required for burial,

scattering, whatever. Some hang about here a long time. Surprisingly heavy, you don't want to drop one on your foot. I have a line of conversation prepared, but she gets in first.

Been busy? Lorelle says.

Mental. You?

Same. Wedding, Saturday. Sit-down at the Manor and Spa.

Nice.

Very nice.

It's now or never, I think to myself.

Ever heard of the Pamplona bull run? I say. They do it in Spain, July 6th. Dates back to the fourteenth century, I add. I find it interesting. I'm considering doing it myself next year, bit of a laugh, I say. I do speak a little Spanish. Hola.

No. Don't know that one, she says. She checks her watch. I never knew you knew Spanish, she says.

I do indeed. Hola. Como esta? Yo soy un hombre.

Lorelle covers a yawn with her hand. Wow, she says. That's good.

In the nick of time I realise this is all me me me. How about you? I say. Any plans for summer?

Not yet, no, she says. Wait and see, I suppose.

Might put some people off, hanging around with cremated people, but not Lorelle. A true professional she is. I tell her so.

She shrugs. I've seen it, done it, been there, she says.

To look at her you wouldn't think it. Butter wouldn't melt. Respect though, total.

Ever been to Il Terrazzo? she asks.

Rings a bell, I say. Think, think, I think.

51

Italian, she says. Three stars. I know someone who went there last month.

Got it, I say.

I'd love to go there.

Yeah?

What I wouldn't give.

She laughs at herself. She's got a good sense of humour.

Not been before then?

Not as yet, no.

She smiles. She has lovely teeth. It's not all death and misery here.

Sorry, I should have offered to make you a tea, I say. I can brew up in the office.

No time. Got to go, she says. It's all rush rush, she says.

Need a hand? I say. I follow her out to her van.

She checks her phone, slams the door. Flashes her smile.

See you later, Lee.

I lean my arm above the passenger window.

Arrivederci then. Mind how you go.

I watch the van pull away. I give myself a little pat on the back. Not at all bad, Lee Hart, if you do say so yourself.

*   *   *

I am out the back, labelling, checking paperwork. Everything labelled big-time. You can't have a gents Seiko getting muddled with a ladies Swatch, upsetting relatives, messy. The dead are labelled same as newborns, but personal effects can go walkabout unless carefully handled. There are things you wouldn't think of, apart from the usual

52

falsies: teeth, wigs, glass eyes; there's implants, lithium-powered devices, including radioactives and prosthetic limbs. Some people are lethal when it comes to what's concealed inside them. When business is slow we do catch-up jobs: coffins, plaque engraving, orders, re-stocking. Now and then there are quiet times, lulls. Feasts or famines. Last month it was quiet for a week. It's dead around here, says Derek. We all laughed, even Reen.

Mikey cleans and polishes the vehicles. I give him a hand. Gets us out in the fresh air and at his age a helping hand is welcome. We take frequent breaks, due to Mikey's blood pressure warnings. We stand out in the parking bay, survey the darkening sky, the oncoming weather, the houses stretching on and on—left towards the railway line, right towards the High Street. So many houses. Dwellings, Mike calls them. We take it all in. He lights his fag. Over the years each one of these houses will give up their dead.

I am diving down the corridor, lightning-quick, me. Never fear Lee is here.

Sorry I'm late.

A man comes towards me. He walks like someone in bomb disposal approaching a tunnel.

That's alright, Sir. Not to worry.

Not a problem, I say. He doesn't hear me. You use your judgement, when, how. The grieving are not the living or the dead. They are in a place of their own.

I put my hand on his arm. Touch is the language of grief. When a loved one dies you speak it fluent, *bosh*, overnight. This way, Sir. Here we go. Shall we have a sit down? Follow me.

Here we learn to communicate with the bereaved as we go along. Some of us are fluent already. Every one of us in this life speaks it in the end.

Like any language there are rules. My hand mustn't remain on his arm too long else I will have intruded. Too short and it's offhand. Pat the arm and you create the impression this is not a priority for you. Timing. Hands are everything, what you do with them. The worst is hands in pockets, forget it—bad as blowing your nose, clearing your throat and looking at your watch all put together. Death is a high-wire act.

By two o'clock the sky has burst. Pouring. Cats and dogs. Me and Derek are soaked. I've not done Horse-Drawn before. Two black gee-gees, all the trimmings. The driver, Terence, he's rainproofed, all the gear, jammy git. Me and Derek are toppered and tailed, nothing more: drowned rats. Only the coffin is dry and toasty behind us under glass. You *twats*! someone shouts from a white van as it skims by. Me and Derek ignore it. The horses are called Tiff and Toff. One of them takes a crap and it steams in the rain. Howard dashed out this morning to cover the grave. Jacuzzis, Derek calls them when they fill up. Humour is an essential weapon in the undertaker's arsenal. I bear this in mind.

I text Lorelle a joke.

> 2 cannibals r eating a clown. 1st cannibal turns to 2 other and says, does this taste funny 2 u?

Haven't heard back, as of yet.

A man can't survive on that, Irene.

Reen is in charge of the biscuits. She passes round the tin, a giant Christmas special, two each, no more. Derek reckons he is built larger than the rest of us and, due to the physical nature of his work, he should get extra. Reen's not having it.

Fair's fair for all, she says, and slams the lid.

Hands up who likes marzipan, Derek says. He puts up his own hand. Howard is peeling his banana but pauses to raise his hand. Me and Mike do not. Reen, busy hiding the Christmas tin, doesn't bother.

Proves my point, says Derek. That people are split fifty-fifty over marzipan. Love it or hate it, like Marmite.

I don't care for Marmite, Howard says.

Nor me, says Mike.

Doesn't bother me either way, I say.

Proved! says Derek, putting his hand up. I thang you.

Many people don't like cumin, Howard says.

Marzipan, Derek goes on, ignoring Howard, was Henry VIII's favourite sweet thing.

Is that right? Mike seems genuinely intrigued.

As well as apricots and spiced fruit cake, Derek says. I'm talking sweet things not savoury.

How come you know so much about Henry VIII? asks Howard, narrowing his eye, brushing crumbs.

History, says Derek, is a subject of mine. What are we without the past? Nobodies that's who. It's going on under our noses every day. This tea break for example, he says, is history.

It is now, says Howard, standing up. Interview in Two in ten minutes.

I begin to clear the mugs.

I wonder if I should mention my own connection to history. Derek stretches, hoists his trousers, checks his watch.

I am related on our mother's side to James Phipps, I say.

Derek stops, thinks, flicks his head at me.

Come again? he says.

James Phipps. First person in the UK ever vaccinated. Good, eh?

Doesn't ring a bell, he says.

They experimented on him as a kid, I say. And he doesn't get the pox, he survives. Job done.

And you are related to him?

Phipps, yeah. He's my great-great-great—

Any chance of us rejoining the deceased and the grief-stricken? Howard enquires, head around the door.

Skates on, everyone, please, says Derek. How many times have I said it? The dead don't bury themselves.

8

RAIN AND CLOUD AT FIRST BUT DRIER AND BRIGHTER CONDITIONS DEVELOPING

I try to observe, keep alert, so I don't end up like Les, cabbaged in an armchair, fuses blown. The front door slams, quakes the house. I lean towards the window, catch sight of Ned's bony arse vaulting our gate. He is athletic for a knobhead. How is it a deaf man who never checks for oncoming traffic is still alive? He is wearing one of Mum's deerstalker hats and his trackies hang low on his hips. Some old dear will die of shock. An offensive weapon, that's what he is. I should open the window and shoot him. He's quick, though. You've got to wonder what he's running from. No good asking.

It occurs to me that if I go blind we will be the three hear-no speak-no see-no-evil monkeys. As it is, I am the only one with a plan. I am no saint but I am twenty-first century. I can hoover the house, including the stairs, in two and a half minutes flat with the tube attachment, I timed it.

I do ask myself, Lee, what are you doing? I could walk away and never come back. Granted, I could put my foot down. But I would always wonder. This way I know, I don't have to think on, worry, fret. They are here under my feet, getting on my nerves, costing a fortune.

Lee and I have an understanding, she used to say. Lee is my soldier.

That day we stood, me and Ned in the field; she must've been cremated ten weeks or more.

We'd waited for decent weather. He carried her casket, her name was on the plaque. We stood at the edge of the field waiting for the right moment. I wore my red tie. Ned had fastened the top button of his shirt. I read out the prayer. I liked the bit, *risen with healing in his wings*, but the rest went over our heads. Ned watched my lips to listen. His hair blew in his eyes. As the clouds shifted I did it. I couldn't tell if it was the right moment but the light breaking seemed like a signal. The sun was weak but it warmed our necks. Her ashes blew on to our jackets, up our sleeves. We were sixteen and eighteen but Ned knelt down like a little kid. I saw her ashes in his hair. Clinging, I thought. I waited. By the time he stood up the gap in the clouds had closed over.

*   *   *

Our Dad was a plant operator, he specialised in static tower cranes and mobile elevated work platforms. He worked his way up, he used to joke he'd made it to the top of his profession.

He accepted a job in Dalkeith, Midlothian, as plant and maintenance manager, and he came back less and less until he never came back at all. Me and Ned imagined he must have met someone. We decided she was blonde, a dancer we reckoned: Candy, Sheryl. Something like that.

The cranes suited him, our mum said. Alone up there among the clouds where no one could reach him. He spread his wings, stepped off, floated away.

Lester had no skyward leanings. Never mind what might have been, could have been, never was. Les was as plain as the nose on your face.

He took us on day trips: model railways, garden centres, car boot sales. We ate pasties, visited the gift shop. He sang along to Bruce Springsteen in his Ford Mondeo. He made her happy. We kept our opinions to ourselves.

I have wondered if our dad is still alive, swinging among the clouds in a crane cab. She was the only one who could've found out. I have an inkling he is still with us. He must wonder what has happened to his sons, Lee Paul and Ned Joseph. Here we are, Dad. He said to me once, At the end of the day, Lee, you come back down to earth, no matter how high you go.

*   *   *

I remember all our roadkill trophies from back when. Hard won they were. We had to position ourselves very carefully to make a play for the smashed pheasant. It was lying by the central reservation, torn like a puppet. I count Ned down for the oncoming traffic. He takes his time. Typical. Reckons himself the expert now. Like this is a useful expertise. Like it'll be his career, scraping up dead things.

He waves at me. Gog! Look at me!

I wave. I jump up and down. Cars are coming. She'll kill me if. Hurry up then. For *fucks*. Come on! Now!

*   *   *

We took ourselves out when she was bad, when she was weepy. Take our minds off. Get some fresh air. The doctors, the mastectomy, the chemotherapy,

59

had all worked then failed. She made a new plan. She was in charge of plans in those days. We all agreed the new plan would work a treat, even Les. The new plan involved a new approach. To help us all understand it there were leaflets offering advice, information, facts.

I took money from her purse. Me and Ned bought sandwiches and crisps at the garage. I read a leaflet while we ate the crisps.

The single most important key to surviving advanced CANCER is working with an expert who knows fighting advanced cancer is like fighting a raging house fire! You cannot fight it with 5 or 6 garden hoses. You need firemen!

Lester was her fireman. Day and night down the pole. Peeling, chopping, dicing, grinding the juicer. He drove her to a place for doses of intravenous vitamin C, a place for intravenous vitamin B17. A clinic where they plugged her in, like Frankenstein's monster, to a Frequency Generator. Les read the leaflet. I read the leaflet. Ned read the leaflet. **Electromedicine produces miraculous results!** You can't argue with that. **A machine that turns cancer cells to normal cells. When used with a water ionizer,** it says, **the process allows clusters of water to get inside cancer cells, detoxifying dead microbes and the toxins they create**. Result. Impressive. Ned steals one of my crisps. I kick him.

The vast majority of alternative CANCER treatments out there are *garden hoses*. We will supply you with the *fire hoses* you need for both home and clinical treatment. Survival means acquiring 3 things!! (1) At least 1 fire hose. (2) Several garden hoses. (3) An expert to work with patient and/or caregiver.

60

You can't take it all in, it's too scientific. We take extra copies of the leaflet to read at home. We walk home the long way. I used to prefer to get home after dark, after she'd fallen asleep. If we were lucky we would hear the owl hooting, just like when we were little kids, same old, as if nothing had changed.

9

SOME OUTBREAKS OF LIGHT RAIN AND INTERMITTENT
DRIZZLE EXPECTED IN THE AFTERNOON

Les remains in his TV armchair, finger on the remote. We all know Raven is here. He is at the kitchen window, hair standing on end in the crosswind. He never uses the door, we don't bother wondering why. He goggles at us through the glass, babbling on, as if we can hear him. Ned could translate, should he choose to read Rave's lip-flapping. He doesn't. Everything is always me. I let him in because no one else will. Never has a family group ignored each other more, I don't even bother pointing it out. It's like we're in separate jars in a museum.

We've got a door you know, I say.
A new one? Rave asks as he steps in.
Ned lays his head on the table.
How do, sirrah? says Rave.
Tea? I say.
If you're making.
What's new? says Rave.
Nothing. You?
Grief, strife.
Les has not yet torn his gaze away from the TV. Rave could be wearing a Superman costume for all he knows.
Ned closes his eyes. Rave sits down and reads our fuel and electric bills that are lying on the table.
Two sugars? I say.
Please, says Rave.

I'll have coffee, Les says to the TV.

When I go they might as well bury me with a kettle, I say.

No one replies.

When you're in the tundra your blood freezes at between –2 and –3 degrees Celsius, Rave says.

I wait while the kettle boils. Is it cold out then?

No.

Blind leading the blind. Love it, Lester informs the TV.

I notice Rave's trainers.

New?

Rave lifts his foot.

Nike clearance. Thirty-eight quid.

Aware of a switch in focus, Ned lifts his head.

Greetings, Noddy Nedmund. How goes it? Rave mouths slowly. Ned drops his head again, shuts his eyes. He read the words fine, but he won't bother.

Have a little sleep, Rave says, patting Ned's shoulder. Nighty-night. Sleep tight. Bloke fainted at work on Tuesday, I wasn't there, Rave says.

Milk? I say.

Thanking you kindly, maestro. One of them immigration things.

Right.

I'm going to have to go to the dentist with this tooth, Rave says. You sold up yet?

No. Valuation first.

Have I died or has no one made me a cup of coffee? Les asks the TV.

Rave slurps his tea.

Had your hair cut, Lethal?

If I had a pound for every time I've said that! shouts Les.

I check my reflection in the chrome kettle, my

63

giant head and tiny body and the room stretching into an endless corner behind. If another dimension did actually exist, for real, I'd go there in the blink of.

I wash the mugs, then we walk to the mast, me, Rave and Ned. Out for a stroll. Windy. Each time I look back at the house I picture it exploding in flames, Les still inside it.

We stop at the mast. Raven makes an observation.

All those people talking to each other, he says, but here at the phone mast, silence.

Me and Ned don't add anything. Rave has said it all really.

Raven's cone of hair erects in the wind. We laugh.

Fuck off, Rave says, but he waves it about.

Dickhead, we say.

We walk up to the woods. Ned follows. No sign of Crow. Shy are we today?

The wind shivers the trees, throws a spring in your step. Ned runs off, returns with grass stains on his clothes.

I feel proud of the woods, as if I made them myself. As we walk, I reckon they are mine by claim. These others are my guests. Would you like to see my woods? Be my guest.

We sit by the oaks. Rave lights a Camel and Ned cadges one.

Can I have one? I say.

Only four left.

Tightarse.

He chucks it. I dive to catch it in my mouth.

Missed!

Cheers, you knob.

Ned laughs.

I have always caught cigs first time. A rare miss there by me.

Nice to have a smoke. Sunlight falls through the trees and lands on us, strobing, warming us up. Smoke drifts. It's like we are hunters and this is our base camp.

I hear Crow at last.

Nice base camp, Lee.

Cheers, Crow. Welcome to Lee's Wood.

No one says anything else. I reckon I am happy. Definition of happiness: When knob-all happens but you don't mind in the least. Can't last of course, nothing does.

10

ANY CLOUD IN THE SOUTH OF THE REGION WILL SOON
MOVE AWAY, LEAVING A DRY DAY

Derek is pacing up and down in the workshop in front of the Mid Oak Veneers. His gut leads the way.

One and two and one and two, he counts, like a bride down the aisle, a pregnant one. The *and* gives you the timing, he says. Are you with me? Otherwise you'll be off like a steamed cat. Nerves, Lee. Empty your mind, he says. Bit like ballroom dancing, he says, without the music or the twists and turns, or the partner. Got it? Off you go.

I feel like a bona fide twot. Coffins are empty but. I get an idea of a smirking client inside each. Derek counts me, One *and* two *and*.

I got a text this morning from Lorelle in response to my joke. It was brief. It said, He he. That was it. Nothing more. Beggars can't be choosers. Least she replied, he he. I'm not cut out for this. Leading the coffins calls for a certain type, an extrovert. Derek or Howard for example. I am not of that ilk.

Slower, Lee.

All eyes are on the page for a start. He leads on. Everyone looks. No thanks. This is why I don't dance. I don't take to the floor, not even at weddings.

And two. Slower!

I keep my eye fixed on the corner of the room where the spiderwebs hang. *Tough Guys Don't Dance*, I never saw that movie. No idea what it's about.

You look like a fascist, Lee.

This will be over in a minute. I'll be deemed unfit. He he.

Derek runs a tight team. My lads, he calls his pall-bearers, though the youngest is fifty-nine. He won't have them mucked about, protective he is. I don't want my lads injured, he says. If the vicar gets slow in front, Derek bumps him gently with the coffin to speed him up, save the bearers.

A marathon around some of these churchyards, Derek says. You'll hear about it if one of my lads goes down, he says. We are men, not machines.

Finally, Derek stands.

Right. That's enough, son. Either got it or you haven't. Grieve ye not. It's not *Strictly Come Whatever*.

Sorry, Del, I say. Turn a new *page*, I say. He he, I think. But he doesn't get it.

There's a removal to do.

Where?

The nursing home. When shall I tell them?

Be at least an hour. An hour at least. Do you mean Elmwood?

That's it. I'll say three o'clock, half past three OK?

No problem. Shouldn't be a problem.

I'll tell Mike. The rear car park. That's what she said.

Okey-dokey. Got it. Rear entrance. Half past. What you laughing at?

I text Lorelle another joke, something to brighten her day.

67

Hola! Como esta? What beats his chest and swings from cake 2 cake? Tarzipan. He he! Mind how u go. Lee.

Howard is back from the motorcycle funeral and is having a lie down in Relatives 2. Give me a biker's funeral any day. Game on. We use 2wheels2heaven, a reliable outfit with a nifty website. You name it, they've got it: Triumph, Suzuki, Harleys. All bikes are modified with the hearse attachment which travels sidecar plus all are constructed to UK funeral profession specifications. Talk about top-drawer. The hearse has all mod cons: flower rail, wraparound windows, internal temperature control, de-mister, internal lights and special cubbyhole to display the deceased's boots. Nice one. They've thought of everything, including a pillion seat for the funeral director. I fancy the Triumph hearse; tasteful, though Howard may beg to disagree. They did the ton, apparently, on the A22 road heading north. Final wishes of the deceased, you can't not. You'd have thought being a Tour de France fan Howard would've been fine, but no. It was a blur, he says. Irene's gone out for paracetamol.

Derek's an expert on pacemakers. He's done loads, a boxful he's got. They have made him famous. Derek and the Pacemakers. Someone wrote it on the workshop wall with permanent marker. It stuck. Derek wrote, Ho Ho Ho, underneath with a biro. Reckon he approves.

Got to know what you're doing with a pacemaker, removing one is like bomb disposal. It will throw a man across a room. Heavy they are, hold one in your hand you won't believe it; steel padlocks running thick steel wires, two or four depending. Cut the wires one at a time, cut two and you'll get a nasty kick. We get several a year, the doctor always mentions when there's one fitted. He better had, else that'll be the end of the crem. Kerboom. Derek cuts them out of the left shoulder, wrapped in plastic they are; no blood, just fat, very clean. He keeps them in a box on the workshop shelf. Batteries from all my broken hearts, he once said. That got me thinking. Where they will all go in the end who do know?

I deliver two teas and a coffee, white with two sugars. On the settee is a man so thin you reckon you're nodding buenos dias to a grasshopper. Beside him his giant wife has to stretch her legs out either side of the coffee table. I have a technique where I hold the door with my foot while I swing the tray through. Howard insists on the wooden tray even though it's cumbersome to manoeuvre. He says the flowery tray is too flippant for the Relatives' Room.

Excuse the interruption. I always say that. Relatives have the opportunity to take a breather, sit back, think on.

The wife has our music menu on her knee. Celine Dion and Whitney Houston are still reigning supreme after years at the top of the crematorium charts. Also up there are Frank Sinatra, Perry Como, the Three Tenors and Freddie Mercury. 'Candle in the Wind', since Diana died. The Commodores and Barry White for the romantics. Then you've got your more traditional 'Abide With Me', 'Amazing Grace', etc. and your show songs from *Les Misérables, Lion King* and *Pirates of the Caribbean*. The vast majority of dead individuals are over sixty. Our menu goes by genre: Popular, Easy Listening, Classic Rock, Country, Jazz. Most people like a bit of music. You do get the occasional Meat Loaf or Aerosmith.

While I set out cups and enquire how many sugars, Howard uses the time to fan the catalogues, display examples. The Cloud Visions range, he says, can customise to a T. You name it they can produce it. They did a bespoke golf bag for a gentleman, he says, hand-crafted, with five-irons on the lid and his initials and a specially engraved plate, entirely unique. Cloud Visions are the last word in bespoke coffinry, they can do all sorts. A broad selection is available, all tastes catered for: football teams, horse racing, animal prints, the Lake District.

There is a photo of the golf bag coffin in the bureau top drawer in case a relative expresses interest. About three out of ten relatives do express interest and Howard jumps to it. No one has, as yet, placed an order but never say never.

The lack of a decent golf course in the area is the explanation according to Howard. Golfers tend to go to W. D. Brookes Funeral Services at the top of the High Street. This is a pity, Howard says. According to him W. D. Brookes is a rip-off, sheer snobbery, one-upmanship. Adam's fireplaces and original cornicing turns people's heads, he says; as in life in death. You get your money's worth here, he says.

True, but some would rather have the icing on the cake. It's a status thing. Most people don't want to go to Heaven in a bag, even if it is bespoke.

Howard still dreams of the day we will get a

full-blown affair, a proper ten- to fifteen-grander, customised everything, no holds barred. He is waiting for someone to push the boat out. You can't blame him because this is his be-all and end-all—his first, his last, his everything, as Barry White likes to sing down at the crem.

Newsflash. A text from Lorelle has landed.

He he he! C u l8er. L.

A definite improvement on He he. More than twice as many words. A step in the right direction, I'd say. Meanwhile, on the subject of love, Derek has some advice. Standing there stirring his tea: Date a midwife, he says. Same type of graft, he says, same hours, same wavelength. Off he strolls, leaving me gobsmacked, holding the kettle. Cheers, then.

We are even stevens today. Four gents, four ladies. Mrs Lomax is being viewed later. Good afternoon, Mrs Lomax, I say.
     Talking to yourself again. Sign of madness. Where's my screwdriver? Derek doesn't stop for an answer. His waistcoat and collar are undone; his face is shiny after only minutes in the workshop. One day he'll topple into one of the coffins and that will be that. Talk of the town then. He wouldn't mind, chuffed probably. Picture in the *Advertiser*.
     Death is expensive. Cheaper to stay alive. Unless you're Derek, with his weakness for patisserie items and baked goods.
     I've worked all my life, he says, and all I've got to show for it is this gut.

Derek is a contradiction in terms, he can be light on his feet when he wants to. The only time things get hairy is when we've got a rush on. No one's fault, but it can get a bit brisk. I only saw Derek lose his grip once, not the whole gentleman, just the top half. I don't like it when clients get a knock, especially the head. You feel bad, but it can happen when there's a rush on. Can't be helped. You apologise. Very sorry about that, Mr Anderson, you say. That was his name.

We are magicians, Derek says, but not miracle workers. Our task is impossible, he says. Our task is necessary. He waggles his fingers in the air, then he says, Fetch me a magic wand, Lee.

*   *   *

Lorelle's van is parked up. Olé. No sign of her. I lean on the van, arms out, wait for her to mosey along. I think on. I remember my hair. I lean in quick, check in one of the wing mirrors.

All right, Lee?

Whoa. How-do. Hello-hello. What brings you here this fine day?

Same as usual. Flowers.

Flores, flora, florals. How's it going?

Fine, thanks. You?

Pretty good, I say. All pretty damn good here at the ol' ranch.

Great. Gotta go, Lee. See ya.

She opens the door, climbs in. I jump around to slam the door for her.

God, Lee. No need to wham it.

Sorry about that. Don't know my own.

Bye then.

I watch the van until it veers around the corner, out of sight.

Arrivederci, mi amore.

My luck's in. I can feel it.

11

A DRY EVENING, WITH SOME CLEAR SPELLS AND
CLOUD INCREASING THROUGH THE NIGHT

She found websites based in America, Mexico,
Australia. She sat at her screen day and night. No
fat, no animal protein, no milk. She ate only fruit,
berries, vegetables, like someone visiting from the
Stone Age. This was the true path, she said. It's up
to me. I can cure myself if I choose. It comes from
within, she said.

We found ourselves wading in information.
Pamphlets, cuttings, leaflets, keeping us in the
picture. **Many foods feed cancer cells! Other foods
virtually destroy the energy of almost all cells!
Starve the cancer cells!**

Giant containers of distilled water stood stacked
in the kitchen for cooking, rinsing, washing. Ned
carried them in one at a time. No plastic wrap or
tinfoil allowed because they were the enemy. Old
fillings and **cavitations** were also a cause of breast
cancer. Who knew? Who would've guessed? You
start to see cancer lurking in everything. Up and
down the motorway she went with her fireman,
Les, at the wheel. Dental appointments, oxygen
treatment, ozone treatment, hydrogen peroxide.
She knew to stay away from qualified doctors at
all cost. The evil white coats of the NHS. Everyone
knows their game. A plotting tribe of neo-fascist
bullies, she called them; she got that off a herbalist.
Not just that. The pharmaceutical companies
want profits not cures, she said. And there was

74

evidence. The aromatherapist at the clinic who had discovered how to successfully shrink tumours using her own patented breathing techniques, had been threatened, burgled, bombed. By who? Mercenaries hired by the major pharmaceuticals. It was a disgrace, a scandal, a conspiracy; a famous naturopath said so. The cat was out of the bag. **Remember: Your doctor has NOT been trained in using natural substances in the treatment of disease.**

I lay with her on the settee. Her eyes are closed. I hold her hand. It's the expense of the treatments, she says, that's the worry. This makes me laugh.

Arseholes, I say. Skanks. Knobs to that. This makes her laugh.

On this me and Les agree. Never mind the cost if it works, he says.

Course it works. This is the miracle path. **Stay positive! Be cured!** She was a survivor, she would fight. She would cure herself by working with nature, not against it. There were a billion vitamins available on the internet, she just had to find the right ones. **If you live long enough to take full doses of our potent cancer treatment for** TWO MONTHS **there is a very good chance you** WILL **beat your cancer!**

A good chance, good enough. Belief was everything. She believed. We believed. We became a family of believers overnight.

A few years before her cancer was diagnosed, Les performed the duties of our local Cancer Research charity shop's Christmas Santa. As a member of the Laughing Mask Players he offered his services each year. He stood with his charity bucket on the High

Street shouting, 'Tis the season to be jolly. Fa la la la la la la la la! The life and soul, our mother called him. This is not what me and Ned called him, but we didn't want to spoil it with our niggling doubts.

He slipped an arm around her waist. Everything to play for, Les always used to say, like he had a dice in his hand. He assumed his position as head of the family. His optimism was embarrassing.

Whoever's with me, say Aye! he used to call. Ned and me were left with no alternative.

Aye, I replied.

He was nervous of Ned. He spoke through me as if Ned was an alien: Tell him it's on the table. Ask him is that a tattoo on his neck or dirt? If I speak like this, s-l-o-w-l-y, will he know what I'm saying?

No, Les. He's deaf not stupid.

He began to get shirty with me.

Lee. That's a girl's name, isn't it?

He had a decent singing voice, granted. He admired Bruce Springsteen, Tom Jones. He had a lust for life. He had bonhomie when the mood took him. He liked to throw his arms wide, *What's New Pussycat!* and take you by surprise.

Don't get me wrong, Lester was decent to her, she allowed him to sweep her off her feet, albeit to a Harvester Inn. It's just that she could've done better. In my humble opinion.

You don't sign as well as him, do you, Lee? Don't worry. I wasn't my mum's favourite either, he said.

A sharp tongue he had. Bodysnatcher, he called me when I got the trainee position.

Look out. Bodysnatcher's about.

This was before.

Then her diagnosis, then her prognosis. Lester

76

announced we would fight it as a family, he stood up to say it. He sold his caravan, a Buccaneer Elan, and bought a Coachman Pastiche, a five-berth tourer with carpet, oak fitted cupboards, ample seating, double glazing and a sun awning. He stuck his head through the little window and shouted, The whole of the UK is ours for the taking! like he was Dick Turpin. We went to Cornwall in the June and then he sold it before Christmas to fund her treatments. There's always another caravan, he said. Respect for that. Some of us only earn respect after death. Better late than never.

For example, I knew a kid at school, Daniel Atkinson. A nobody. A zero. Dies unexpectedly and hey presto! Instant fame. Fact was he was nothing special, no one rated him. Then, soon as he was gone he became an overnight sensation. Belter of a funeral. Everyone had a story, everyone knew his name. If only I could have remembered something, anything about Daniel. I remembered his shoes, the same black Barratts as mine except his rolled in. And his name came after Paul Aldiss on the class register. I wished we'd had a conversation or a fight. I can't remember anything he said or did or even his voice. Or even his face. When his name comes up I always mention that I was at school with him. People are surprised, sympathetic. I knew him, I say, same class, same age, same time. Terrible, I say. The exact same shoes. Tragic. He came second on the class register. His grave is in the churchyard by the yew hedge. His name is carved. Daniel Atkinson became a local superstar. It's living that makes you invisible.

I compose a poem to Lorelle. I have not addressed

Artistic Guy vis-à-vis Five Things Girls Can't Resist. It's now or never, as Derek would say Elvis would sing. Harder than it looks. In the end I go for short and sweet. I send it as an SMS.

> You and me. Just the way we talk, stand around. It keeps my feet on the ground and my head in gear. In the summer sun at this time of year. You and me.

I'm not saying it's Shakespeare, but. Reckon it might touch a nerve, slant things in the right direction. Girls like things to rhyme.

*   *   *

Speaking of girls, Ned has met one online. On Chatroulette, the site where, play your cards right, you'll likely meet a mass murderer or two. Lovely. Her name is Debra-Ann, according to Ned. His hands fly, two birds in a net. Of course this will not be her real name. I sign this to him. Her real name will be Graham, she'll have three bodies under the floorboards, two more in the Ford Transit. Talk about gullible. He finds this funny.

Jealous! Jealous! he signs.

Ned believes anything anyone tells him. Without me he'd be eaten alive. I'd love to see a picture of Debra-Ann. I could admire her piercings, her display of dentistry, her Adam's apple. I wouldn't mind but someone's got to look after him. Ned says he can talk to people online without them having to know he's deaf.

Wear clothes, I tell him, when you chat. Reckon he's more chance of meeting someone sane if he's dressed. Life would be better in general if Ned wore more clothes. He goes shirtless because he's big on sensation, he likes the feel on his skin: wind, water, psychopaths. He goes shirtless in the field, he thinks I don't know.

He falls asleep like a cat. He curls up anywhere. Ned can bend himself any which way, God's gift to yoga, a waste really. He is spark out on the settee, mouth open. Silence is golden. Sausage casserole we had, my own recipe. Plates are drying on the drainer. I am concerned lately that he has maybe joined an online cult. He has begun to smirk and grin at inappropriate times, as if he's some kind of enlightened soul. Arsehole, more like. Let's face it, he is easy prey for wackos.

As well as communicating with nefarious psychotics online and staring at naked girls, Ned also spends time on air disaster sites: emergency landings, near misses, crashes, you name it. What would poleaxe you and me lights him up like Christmas. He can't see the horror, don't ask me why. He can watch those planes skid, spin and break up no problem at all. Like when we scattered her ashes in the field, it's not that he doesn't feel it, he just sees another side. To him normal everyday things are madness and vice versa. Like he's looking down the wrong end of a telescope.

I let myself out. Quiet. Birds beginning to roost. No wind. Decent moon up. The field is full of rabbits, as I walk they flow away, puts me in mind of locusts. I have never seen a locust except on TV. I climb the stile, walk the set-aside. Pigeons in a corner of the field. They rise up, clatter clatter, and swerve towards the woods. I turn my attention to the mast instead.

Greetings, mast. Buongiorno.

Me and the mast have a lot in common. We stand tall in all weathers, no funny business, no shirking, no day off. No one notices. No one thinks what if the mast/Lee didn't exist. Then what?

I stroll towards the lane. I have a gander. I don't think it's right, some Nordic knob chasing an A-level student on a public highway, ditto GCSE, it makes no difference. It's not on, that's all I'm saying. If I see anyone suspicious I'll have a word.

The lane is empty. Just Crow laughing his head off. Private joke, I assume. I leave him to it.

I can't put my finger on what's gone wrong in my life. Mainly it's Ned. Not his fault per se, he's just a pain in the arse. He wasn't born deaf. At four months old he caught measles off me. She set up his crib beside her bed and watched him through the bars. I remember his cry, like one of the farm strays.

I used to spy on them through the door crack, wishing she would come back to me, watch me sleep instead, wishing I was iller than him.

By the time he was seven months old she had to admit Ned was deaf as a result of his bout of measles. We were not inoculated. The GP told her it might be permanent. It was.

A poison cocktail, she called the MMR vaccine. A time bomb. No one knows what's safe, she said. The doctors are experimenting on our children.

This was all about baby Tom from her childhood. I reckoned it so. I'd put money down. As a kid she'd played with baby Tom's big sisters, up Copthorne way. After he was born, baby Tom had been given the whooping cough vaccination from a toxic batch and was brain damaged. Everyone in the village knew. All the mothers nattered about it. She still went on about it and baby Tom's mother, all these years on; a saint, she called her. Over twenty years back but fresh in her mind. Things can haunt you just as well as ghosts. For our own protection we weren't inoculated; as far as she was concerned the doctor's verdict that vaccinating me would have protected Ned was rubbish. She liked a good ruckus with a person in charge.

Deafness is not a disease, she told the doctor at the surgery. There's nothing wrong with my son. Ned is a clever boy, hearing or deaf, she said. And no, she would not consider a cochlear implant or a hearing aid, not now or ever. You can't force me, she said. I have rights.

So does he, the doctor said.

I stared at the doctor. I took my time. I thought about punching him. Smashing his face into his desk. Breaking his nose, splitting his lip. Talking to her that way. She refused to sit on a chair, she gripped my hand instead, swaying, head high. I am a mother, she told him, I know what's right.

The doctor rubbed his eye as he spoke. The vaccination works, he said, it protects children. He sounded at his wits' end.

There is evidence that the vaccine is unsafe she replied. It will probably be proved, she added. I have done the best for my boys. We shall see, won't we?

She had the last word. She swept out, leaving all the doors open, like royalty. I was proud. She stood up to him. She was a warrior. And the fact that my brother was deaf was not my fault in any shape or form. No way was I to blame. She said so.

She never mentioned baby Tom. I didn't know why then but I do now, no one likes to admit to ghosts, it's like admitting you are afraid.

She waited for her day to arrive. Then in 1998 it did. Andrew Wakefield declared the MMR vaccine was responsible for autism. She bought a bottle of red wine and we toasted her in the kitchen while she cooked spaghetti.

Hallelujah! she said.

We gave her three cheers. Hip hip! While Ned looked silently on.

You were saved, she said, holding my face in her hands, by the skin of your teeth.

Thanks, I replied.

She loved us. Let sleeping dogs lie.

*   *   *

When the alarm goes off I do not get a sinking feeling. Raven says his heart sinks every single day. I would rather go to work than stay here, listening to trampoline twangings. I have borrowed Raven's hair mousse. RokHard, it's called. It will do the job re my wavy fringe. I can't see Lorelle going for curls, frankly. Speaking of which. I have not heard a dicky bird. I am concerned the poem has muddied the waters. I text her again.

Hey u. howdy. having fun? sorry not been in touch. total madness here! c u soon. Lee.

The clouds are low today, everything drips from the morning's rain. On my way back from the crem in the hearse I have a brainwave.

Just drop me here, I tell Mikey. I can walk back.

Just got to check a floral order, I tell him.

Right you are, he says.

I have a gander through the glass before I go in. Not a curl to be seen on my whole head. Ding goes the bell. The room is cool, empty, perfumed with the smell of flowers.

Hello, can I help you?

It's not Lorelle. It's Jan, the other one.

Howdy, Jan. No, I was just wondering if Lorelle was about.

You just missed her by two minutes, not even. Can I give her a message?

No, it's all right. Yes, OK. Just tell her Lee was passing and says, Buenos dias.

Okey dokey. How are you spelling that?

I prefer to walk, given the option. You miss so much in cars. There is a weeping willow by the postbox grown over the fence, a group of starlings circling over the old schoolhouse. I see the milk float parked. I often see the milkman. We had a conversation about asteroids once. I do not know his name, even though we discussed the universe at length. Change is in the air. I can feel it in my bones.

Irene's got the fan heater on in the office.

Hello, Lee. What have you done with the sunshine?

I find Derek sitting on a Winchester Mid Oak Veneer eating a bacon butty.

Get that kettle on, son.

I find Mikey to ask if he wants a brew. He is still sitting in the hearse in his anorak, reading the *Sun*.

Young man, you're a star, he says.

83

I take Howard his usual coffee, one sugar, two biscuits. He is checking his tie in the mirror. He sees me in the mirror. Teethfest.

Hello there, Lee. All right? Have you cut your hair? You look different.

12

A DRY START, WITH KEEN EAST OR SOUTHEASTERLY WINDS, PARTICULARLY ON SUMMITS

Mrs Grierson is nice and clean except for iodine discoloration. The wound is stitched, taped, neat and tidy. I cover her. Her belly is full, though her baby is at the hospital in his father's arms. I rinse her hair. Lucky to have a natural shine. I pat her face dry. I don't want drips running down. They do of course. They become Mrs Grierson's tears. I am careful with my stitching. It is wrong to close a mother's mouth before she has spoken her baby's name. I stop, I step back. I try to put some distance between but the gap won't widen. Sorry, I say. My voice dings off the metal dish. It was better before when I said nothing. Shut up, Lee. I plug in the hairdryer. I don't switch it on. I sit down. I touch her hand. I hope she saw him. You are not supposed to touch clients unnecessarily. Or think about the circumstances of their death. You are not supposed to mull over, think on, or be maudlin. I touch her fingers. You are not supposed to hold their hand. It's on the list of things considered inappropriate, a step too far. Lee, you have gone too far. Mrs Grierson doesn't seem to mind. Her fingers start to warm under mine. Not to worry, Mrs Grierson, take your time. I am here.

Miss Langley, I presume?
I prefer to greet people my own age with a joke, puts us on a par. Miss Langley's tray flies out on her

runners just as Derek steps in.

Evening all.

The sky is pink over the dual carriageway, turned the pine trees black on the west side; they look like a crowd of mourners. One of them is the total spit of Howard leading on with his silver-topped cane. You can't count on a sunset around here. As I look my phone tings.

Hey u. crazy here 2! L8ers! L.

Reason to be cheerful. Result. I check for hidden meaning. I read it again. Then I read it again. If it was a normal Tuesday I'd meet Raven at The Lion, but he's on Lates this week. Just as well as it happens.

*   *   *

I put the tea on, beefburgers: a treat. I wait for Ned to come down. He likes burgers. Twelve buns, 48p. Bargain. I'll freeze the rest. I take Lester his as usual. It's only as I'm putting it down I notice. I look at him and of course straight away I know. The TV is blaring. Same old, but.

I look at his head, lolled, like one of Ned's pigeons. *Would you like to see inside your house*?

Only then do I notice his eyes. Then the smell.

Les?

I switch off the TV.

I can't think what to do next. Funny. This is my daily bread. If I was going to expect the unexpected it would not be death. Death is my Monday to Friday. Don't bring your work home with you, that's what they say. Too late. I hold my head in my hands.

Take your time, I tell myself. Sit yourself down.
I'm ready when you are.

13

CLOUDY WITH LIGHT RAIN AT FIRST, BECOMING
BRIGHTER AND CLEARER BY THE AFTERNOON

My hands explain it to Ned. *Dead*. My hands flatten. *Dead Les*. I realise this is only the second time I've had to think how to sign the word *dead*.

Ned folds his arms, looks at the floor. I put my hand on his shoulder, same as we do in the Relatives Room. We stand for a bit like that.

Embarrassing. The fact that I didn't twig. Mortifying. Me, a trained professional. Lee Hart, specialist subject: being deceased. There is evidence Lester died some time ago. Around lunchtime? I had a Chilli Texan burrito. It's possible he's been dead all day, or longer. I wish the ground would open up.

We wait while the kettle boils.

Ned wants to bury him in our garden, like a hamster.

No, I sign.

Privately I admire this idea. But. We need to sell the cottage pronto and this is something not to add to an estate agent's particulars: *Garden laid to lawn with beds. Tool shed. Mature tree. Grave: one occupant.*

Ned wants a plan. I'm in charge of plans.

Tree dig us yes, he signs. He sniffs. He folds his arms over his head as if, next, the house might collapse on us. I don't answer. The tree is a sycamore. She loved it. It tilts away from the house at an angle, like the house is afloat, like we're setting off somewhere. Ned presses his hands over his face. Since he was little this is his way: sightless, soundless, locked in. You have to wrestle him to get his attention. He peeks, one eye.

Doctor, I sign.

Ned rolls his eyes, shakes his head. He is frightened. As if we murdered Les, as if. Ned points at the freezer. I close my eyes. Think think think.

Granted it looks bad, a deceased stepfather decomposing in his own front room under the nose of his trainee undertaker stepson, and yes I have my reputation to consider, but. Even if the freezer was empty it would be necessary to fold Les in half, perhaps quarters, or even eighths.

Ned and me eat our dinner in the kitchen. Mince and onion. Silence, except for the squirt of the ketchup bottle. I don't catch his eye and he doesn't catch mine. His hands won't talk, two empty gloves. I intended putting the radio on but I don't bother now. I let him dry for me at the sink after. We watch it get dark. A dog from the farm kicks off barking.

I go upstairs and stand under the shower. I let it be hot. The GP visited Les recently. Recent enough to keep the coroner out of proceedings. When? Week before last? The coroner will know Les was sat dead in his chair for at least twenty-four hours. Less than ideal. When I pull back the plastic curtain the room has vanished in the steam. I am invisible and nowhere. I am someone else in another house living a different life in some other time. The steam evaporates. I am me in the here and now. You can run but you can't hide, Lee. I check myself in the mirror. I look demented. I was good looking once. What giveth? I go downstairs, light-headed. The smell of a clean T-shirt makes me feel sane. Ned is in Lester's chair, watching *Dancing on Ice*, his hand down his tracksuit. He waves me out of the way.

Anything on?

No, says his other hand.

I boil the kettle. I open the back door. The air is cold but pleasant. Fresh, Lester used to call it. I step out on to the path and in the stillness my step is loud. No moon. I never carry a torch, you don't see anything outside the beam. You can see a light from the road, the rest is black.

My name is Lee Hart. In my line of work you get used to it. After a while you stop noticing. The border is no more a border than these fences around here, it's just the other side. Sometimes you forget, the hours can be long, you forget who is alive and who is dead. You have to remind yourself. You wonder if it matters. Sometimes the fence just disappears and you are in no-man's-land.

Next morning I make porridge with salt, like she used to. We will need our strength. Ned watches with big eyes, arms folded, foot jigging. I spread my arms to get his attention. I sign him that we must complete a simple manoeuvre after which everything will be right as rain. A girl could do it, I sign. No problem. Easy peasy.

He throws his hair back, chucks his spoon in the sink, burps.

I raise Lester under his arms. He is stiffened. Ned lifts his feet. Without hands I'm unable to precisely communicate to Ned what I need him to do. You do not want a deceased individual vertical at this stage of the game, whether you knew them when they were alive or not. I exaggerate facial

90

expressions but Ned isn't looking. He's looking at Les, at his margarine mask face and dark hands. For *fucks*. I put my end down. On the plus side he doesn't hear the gurgles and leaks, but I can do nothing about the smell. Finally, Ned looks at me. At last. Buenos dias. Pay attention, Scrotey. Then. One of Lester's shoes slips and the leg thumps to the floor. Ned, holding the shoe, lets out a cat's wail. I count to ten. One knobhead two knobhead three.

Ned chucks the shoe and runs, hand over his mouth. Total spit of one of Lester's TV reality people seeing their new kitchen for the first time. Anyone would think this was all my fault.

You are excused! I shout. Cheers. But he's already with the long-legged ice dancers in their shiny skirts. Same old. Buonasera. Not a problem. Lee is here, as per.

I pick up Les in my arms, like you would your bride on your wedding day. Les carried her this way when she got weak. These very stairs. I would watch as he climbed, puff puff, he went. I hated it when her foot hit the banister. I manage just two stairs now. Les is heavy; he is leaking, he is staring at me. I put him down. I am in charge of plans. I drag him up by the arms on his back. There is no other way. He spills down his front like a baby. Unpleasant, Howard would call it. His head drags and bumps. Needs must. I remember her saying, You're a natural mover, Lee. Would you like to be a dancer?

If she'd had her way we'd all be leaping and twirling with roses in our teeth. Talk about rose-tinteds.

This is working. Job done. Easier on my own.

We all have a cross to bear and mine is knobhead downstairs.

I will need soap, water, kitchen roll, tea towels, cotton wool. I will have to improvise. I put the kettle on. Catch my breath. I roll up my sleeves. I have that Louis Armstrong song in my head. *I see trees of green. Red roses too.* Something something. *For me and you. And I think to myself.*

The GP drives a Volkswagen Polo.

Once in bed, cleaned and plugged, dressed in fresh clothes, Les looks OK in spite of the staining. Discoloration yes, some hypostasis, but supported on pillows in a clean jacket he looks quite approachable, debonair even. His eyes have clouded. For the sake of appearances I stack fifty-pences on each, as we seem to be out of one-pound coins. The GP is nice, friendly. No worries, he says, though he's not from Australia. He remembers me. I see him flick a double-take at the fifty-pences. I decide not to ask if he has change.

I had my concerns, he says. It was on the cards, he says. Don't give yourself a hard time. Your stepfather's problems were significant and various.

Thank you, I say. I tell him I know it's not unusual, per se.

The GP washes his hands. He pronounces Lester dead.

Your stepfather is dead, he says.

Thank you, I say. I dip my head.

The GP and I have an understanding. He writes the certificate. We estimate a time of death. Less than the actual. Nothing is said vis-à-vis Lester having died approximately forty-one hours ago. If he sees there is evidence, he doesn't let on. He tells

92

me I have done a good job laying out Lester. It's a dying art, he says.

I watch Derek and Mike walking slowly up our path, professional, as if they're at work. A knock. I open the door. They are supposed to say, Good afternoon, Mr Hart. Shakespeare and Son. May we come in? But they don't. No one says anything. Then Derek says, Shall we put the kettle on, son? And they step inside.

They stand in our kitchen. Mike goes outside for a smoke. Derek says, Any biscuits?

I introduce Ned as the kettle boils. Derek and Mike watch my hands signing what is being said so that Ned understands.

You look nothing like each other, Derek says. I sign this too to Ned. He looks away. Mikey says nothing.

I've never before gone by vehicle to work. Funny. A different perspective. The hearse is wide as the lane. I try not to think about Les zipped up in a bag behind us. What's done is done. I put it out of my mind and look out at the sky and trees and hedges floating past. I try to imagine I am a stranger here.

I sit on the settee in the Relatives Room. I am a Relative. Should I ask myself whether I want tea? Coffee? Sugar? Milk?

Tea, Lee? Coffee?

It's Mikey.

This is all wrong. I do the teas and coffees, not Mike. This is wrong, I say.

You're all right, mate, he says. Perfectly normal reaction. Do some deep breaths.

Mike has misunderstood. I nod.

I know the catalogues off by heart. I don't know what Lester would want, we never talked about it. It's a decision for the Relative. That's me. I opt for cremation: The Basic Coffin. Blue satins. Compton Ashes Casket. Embalm no. Crucifix no. Dressed: Own clothes. Viewing: TBA. Personal Effects: TBA. At Rest.

I choose the Sympathy Basket from Fleurtations. I ask to speak to Lorelle personally.

Howard puts his head round the door. I have put my head around that door countless times.

We can do the employee's discount, Howard says. No problem. Comes out very reasonable. He sits beside me. He pats my hand, like I've patted so many hands before.

All right, Lee. Take your time. Anything else you need at all?

No thanks, Howard. Thanks anyway. Where's Derek? I say.

Don't worry, Lee, he says. We'll take care of everything.

Lester is naked on the table when I walk in. Derek jumps in between, tries to hide everything by spreading his arms.

It's OK, Del. I'm fine. Let me help.

No need, Lee. I got it sorted. He lowers his voice, winks. Go and relax till I've got him ready. Don't fret, son. I'll give you a shout.

Behind him Lester's mouth is frozen in a yawn. Bored rigid he looks. An extreme makeover all his own, at last.

*   *   *

Things are almost normal today, Thursday. Lester is prepped, tucked up on his tray in the chiller. I don't open it. The crem is booked.

Early this morning I heard Derek in the workshop on the Gravograph, stapling satins, tapping in coffin handles: door locked. Tomorrow me and Ned are to view Lester in Chapel 1, bid arrivederci. What I'll say to him I do not know.

Miss Langley is still with us. Out she comes on her runners, good as gold. Pulmonary arrest it says on her paperwork. Many of us are walking time bombs.

I'm all right on my own, I tell Derek. You've no need. I'll get on.

Sure? he says.

Sure.

Sunset Glow, Derek says and leaves.

I look at Miss Langley. Never fear, Lee is here. I take out the box of tricks: the combs, the cosmetics, the hairdryer. When you get them so as they look as if they might open their eyes and speak, you're done.

14

CLOUDY AND DULL, WITH SOME LIGHT RAIN OR
DRIZZLE AT FIRST AND SUNNY SPELLS LATER

No sign of Ned this morning. Normally he drops
past the kitchen window on to the trampoline in
time for breakfast before I leave. Shreddies he has,
or Cheerios.

He found the old washing line, the one we used
to play with. Talk about gobsmacked. I had no idea
he even remembered. Need it. Busy. Go away, he
signed. God knows. He slammed his door before I
could ask.

Not your average nine to five, undertaking.
Death doesn't look at his watch. A late finish, dark
by the time I make it to Somerfield to pick up
something for our tea. I choose Somerfield Special
Chow Mein. Lester didn't care for oriental food,
but me and Ned are now free to sample the flavours
of the East. I buy extra noodles. Two cheeky cans of
Stella find their way into my basket, I knoweth not
how.

There's no point calling, I'm home! I say
it anyway. I mosey to the kitchen, unpack the
shopping by the sink, same as. Four minutes in the
microwave on high.

There is a card on the sideboard. *In Sympathy*
it says. *Dear Lee, I'm so sorry for your loss*. Lorelle
has got beautiful curvy handwriting, artistic. *Please
let me know if there's anything I can do*. Well, well.
Buonasera, señorita. As a matter of. Knock it off,
Lee, back in your box. A time and a place.

Quiet. No TV blaring. I open the back door, let myself out. I crack open one of the Stellas. The stone bench under the window reminds me of our mother. She found it in a reclamation yard. I sit on it. It's got a broken griffin at one end.

She used to write messages to herself. She stuck them on Post-Its all over the house. We read them daily. New ones appeared as the old ones fell off. *I am a conqueror. I choose hope. God is not finished with me yet. Healing wisdom . . . Get some!* Every surface of the house was papered with information, the information that held the secret to the cure. They were in capitals, underlined. That's how important they were.

Cancer is caused by imbalance! The logical way to SOLVE this is to use NATURAL Products to safely Target <u>and</u> Kill cancer cells! (E.g. laetrile, found in apricot kernels)!

She signed up for acupuncture, kinesiology and light therapy. And she was happy because happiness too was a cure. **Stress AND sadness cause cancer!** She smiled and laughed. She had a whale of a time, because if you don't laugh you'll cry and months of detoxing and oxygenating will be out the window.

On the walls, mirrors, kitchen cupboards: **Reclaim your inner terrain!** We took note. **The only thing that can let you down is your ATTITUDE.** We adjusted our attitudes. We did everything the leaflets said. We obeyed the pamphlets. We banished sadness. We said the affirmations. We believed. The cancer didn't stand a chance.

*　　*　　*

I put the tea on. Ned is outside, bouncing. He has a look of surprise on his face, like he's trampolining against his will. The twangs are the comedy sound of things going pear-shaped—our theme tune—like some kids' cartoon, *The Knobs*.

Ned's benefit money is going to cease unless he gets a job pronto. We no longer have Lester's disability allowance. My plan is to spend twenty pounds a week less. New world, new rules, same old us. I am not unduly worried. I have a plan. We don't use central heating but we need to pull back in the area of electrics. In the area of food I have come up trumps, if I say so myself. But. I do require an Italian fund, needs must. In this one area I cannot scrimp. It will have to be in the region of one hundred pounds. Undercover Lee has done his research and Il Terrazzo is around about fifty squids a head, plus wine. So far I've got about twenty-nine in the pot. Well on the way. Tulips. Tiptoeing. Sorted, dare I say.

*   *   *

We stand in Chapel 1 looking at Lester in his box. I guessed I would be tongue-tied and I was right. I talk to dead men all day long. Funny. When he was alive I spoke one-way remarks to Les twenty-four seven. Only difference now is the small matter of a pulse. Then there is Ned. He presses his lips together, stares. He looks like a fish out of water. He has never been at my work before. I loaned him my other suit jacket. He slipped it on over his Simpsons T-shirt. You can still see Homer's surprised yellow mug peeking out between the lapels.

We have now studied Lester's face longer than

ever before. A decent job by Derek. He has used plenty, I can see, to cover the darker staining. Typical Les, sloping off without warning. Sod off to the rest. *Don't go away* they say on *Extreme Makeover* during the ads, and he didn't. He went nowhere, but he buggered off just the same. Why not other people's reality if you're sick of your own? Fair play. This real enough for you, Les? Lying here covered in make-up with us two knobs looking on.

I have nothing to say. Zipped, I am. Les has arrivederci'd leaving us none the wiser. One time alive as if he were dead and now dead as if nothing had changed. Buenos noches.

Ned leans in. He touches Lester's arm, his hand. Examining it. I don't recall Ned ever touching Les. Or vice versa. I don't remember any of us touching any of us come to think of it. Ned lowers his head till it lies on Les's chest. I check the door. I'm not embarrassed, per se. I don't know what I am. Looks like he's listening for a heartbeat except (a) Ned is deaf and (b) Les is dead. The blind leading the blind. Les would have loved it.

I don't feel anything much, I wait but nothing comes. I notice the picture of the lakeside sunset is askew so I step over to straighten it. When I turn back Ned is upright again, like he never listened to nothing on Les's chest. Like I imagined it. Maybe I did.

I replace Lester's lid before we leave.

15

MILD WITH STRONG WINDS, GRADUALLY EASING
THROUGHOUT THE DAY

Tap tap. I knock and enter. Good morning, Mrs Evesham. Not the finest of days, I'm afraid. Rain just now, but brightening later, I hear. Mrs Evesham died in her sleep. Nice and easy. No fuss or fanfare. She has no idea she's even gone. No clue. Not to worry, Mrs Evesham. Things may look different but to be perfectly frank it's the same old same old. I bet you can't honestly say you even noticed. Am I right?

Derek is in the back, on coffins. I can hear his radio. Howard is at a crem funeral with the others. Nice and peaceful here. Just Irene front of house; now and then you can hear her voice asking, Now why's that happened? Looking at her screen.

Last June Reen said, Lee, you remind me of an attending angel. Everyone laughed. I felt like a knob but I took it as a compliment. She was referring to my presence, my walk. Because there is a style of walk and talk in my line of work that you must perfect if you want to get on. The talk is one thing, slow and soft, as if someone has died, which they have. The walk is another kettle of fish. The walk must be supervisory, sober, but light-footed. Eggshells we call it. Remember, you are not Dracula, Derek says. You learn to walk on eggshells without coming across as a ponce. Egg-shelling is my speciality, hence Irene's comment. If you want to make it to funeral director you have to be the last word in this skill. Then you have to get the voice right. If you are not posh by birth, and no funeral directors are, then you have to learn to speak toffee, like Howard, a few plums in the mouth. People want death to be posh, nice and smart, even though, of all the things we do, it is the most common.

* * *

Outside the sky is flat blue. I drink instant coffee standing up. The clock doesn't tick at all. All I hear is my breathing. Then a wood pigeon, starting his list and forgetting. I sit and look across the field at the mast. I wait for a thought, a feeling. Nothing comes. My mind is blank as, empty as the woods.

* * *

I sit in the room. I'm supposed to be hoovering, but. Here she died. Here Lester lay. Facts unfit for airing in the presence of prospective house buyers, under the rug they must be brushed, pronto.

Framed photographs. Us when we were young. I stare at us. Me and Ned with freckles, gaps in our teeth. Mum and Les, leaning, laughing up at the camera, surprised, sun-kissed. We seem alive, more than we are now. Who are these people and what are they doing? And where have they gone? I lie on the bed.

I wonder if I lie here long enough whether I might slope off too. I close my eyes. I don't mind, make a change. Buenos noches. Adios. Not that it's easy of course. It isn't. Death: the most natural thing in the world is unnaturally tough to do if

101

you're trying too hard. And certainly not if you are clocking it before it's had a chance to clock you. A watched pot, etcetera. Stare death in the face and watch it paralyse. Death would rather take you by surprise, creep up sideways and *bosh*.

16

PERHAPS A BRIGHT START BUT SOON SOMEWHAT CLOUDY, WITH SHOWERY RAIN

The estate agent has organised house viewings but there are no offers as of yet. I am usually at work during house viewings but I always run the Hoover round.

Today is Sunday. There is a viewing. I tidy up. I put daffs in a pot, though they are yet to open. I put mugs on a tray, I put milk in a jug.

I can hear them moving from room to room. I am waiting upstairs, listening. I can hear them in the kitchen below. The voice of the agent, boom boom boom. Silence. I hope he is pointing out the view. Perhaps they are stunned by it.

Boom boom, off he goes again. I hear them moving out of the kitchen back to the lounge. Boom boom boom. Silence. Possibly they are regarding the view from there too and are amazed. The silence goes on too long. They don't like it. They think it's crap. I displayed the condiment giraffes on the dining table. Probably they're trying not to laugh.

Bollocks to this. Making me out like I'm a dick. I do not want to meet them on the landing, on the stairs. I leg it to Ned's room.

He is online, possibly nude, I don't dwell. I walk straight past. I sign as I go.

Trousers. Now. People.

I open his window, climb, drop out through the space. I hit the trampoline below. One bounce, two, and I step quite elegantly off. I head for the mast. I stroll like always, same as. I don't think about them seeing me or if they're watching. I careth not. Be my guest. Fill your boots. I can just imagine the reaction of old Frilly-Ears Boom-Boom.

Ah! There we are. Look. There in the landscape! You can see a genuine rustic knob making his way to the woods for food. Very rare. Don't move, you might scare him. Bit of local flavour for you there. Mostly, they can't afford to live here any more. Very rare indeed.

The house will sell eventually. Some gold-carded gent will bring his architect. Together they will find a way, using steel and glass, to transform our red bricks and tiles, our pine kitchen and oil-fired Rayburn into something more or less. Something else.

Sell we must, but it's Ned who concerns me. Viewings could be derailed. People might be put off. I've told him to stay in his room, told him the estate agent does the walking and talking, but. He'd think it was funny. Typical of him to jinx it for a laugh, to get on my nerves, to keep the house. Who do know?

I ring the agent.

Did you point out the views? I ask.

Of course, he says. Everything will change in the spring, it always does.

OK. No problem. If you say so. Cheers then.

A prediction. I like that. Everything will change in spring. It always does.

*   *   *

I happen to know her name is Caitlin. I have no idea

how she found her way into my head. She works at DFS on the industrial estate. I tell her their car park is always full, even though I've only been once to look at a leather four-seater. Never mind that, she says, climbing on. There are dreams when you know you're dreaming. Game on.

Under her shirt Caitlin wears a leotard, that's novel, I think. They put her on the till, she says, because she was too efficient in the stockroom. I don't know what she means by that and I had no idea there were poppers on leotards. Took me by surprise. Caitlin is a double D cup. Here's mud in your eye. I reckon Caitlin is wasted at DFS. Her talents, I can vouch, would make a dead man blink. I am putty in her hands. I don't put up a fight. Like I say, she's efficient. She deals with me swiftly, like blowing up a raft. Caitlin is the type of girl who always, even in your dreams, has mini-Kleenex about her person. There is no post-coital, time is money and Caitlin steals none, which is why they put her on the till. The clock is always ticking with her, but when she's gone the clock stops dead. Funny. I had no idea I even fancied her. I lie there like one of our clients.

Lorelle. Lorelle. It's you I really want.

*   *   *

I brew up. Me and Derek take five in the workshop. Derek's had his fair share of suicides. Many a hanging, he says. Hanging is the most popular, according to him. Roughly two a year here.

You remember the name of your first suicide, he says. And your first child. Then as the years go by you muddle them up. As in life, he says.

Derek's had five drownings, several overdoses, three jumpers, fourteen hangings and a shotgun. That was the worst, he says. You try to jigsaw them back together. No one views a shotgun death over here, but. If the family request a viewing you have to warn them, gently, then they use their discretion, the more violent the death the more discretion required.

Yesterday we had tortilla wraps for lunch. Derek said he'd never had a meat wrap. I got him grilled chicken, I had smokey barbecue. Derek can get philosophical when he's eating. Life and death, it's all the same, he says. Sometimes I forget which side I'm on, he says. I didn't comment. I know what he means.

I get a rabbit. Olé. Beginner's luck. I saw it under the fence, half in shadow. I aim, thinking, might as well. I steady my arm against the tree, hold my breath. Frankly, I don't expect to hit it. Take my time, reckon it will run. Next thing it's limp, blood on the grass. Clean kill. Nice one. I carry it home. A big buck, heavy. Skull knocks against my knee. Have to swap arms twice. When I get home it is still warm and sticky with blood.

Stew. Rabbit. Nice. I sign Ned.

He strokes the fur, examines the feet.

No, he signs. Slams the bouncy door on his way out. It quivers open.

Knob. He'd eat it if he was hungry.

I reckoned Ned would help. I'm disappointed. It's on eHow: how to skin a rabbit. It would've been good. The brothers Hart and their rabbit dish. There are those who would put it on YouTube. We could've. Why not?

I lay it in the freezer in its fur. Its dark eye stares up, surprised. I close the lid.

Reckon our luck will change any minute. Stands to reason. Nothing stays the same, so. I tidy up, put the tea on. Shepherd's pie, my own recipe, à la baked beans. I would have quite fancied being a shepherd. Wrong area, no sheep. If the farms were still going Ned would have found something by now, the last one was sold off in sections last year and ours went aeons before that. City knobs building weekend homes. Architects in leather coats arriving in wide cars, asking if the pub does decent food. Someone is converting the old barn, paddocks they want, for llamas.

Outside Ned goes up and down on the trampoline. He makes a different shape in mid-air each time. You wonder what the birds think.

The lady rings from the JobCentre to tell us Ned has an interview. A great opportunity, she calls it. Tasty, it sounds. Less than twenty miles away; a fifteen-minute train journey and a short bus ride.

But no.

No way, Gog. No can do. No way, he signs.

He won't even go for the interview. They will get him some counselling, they say, but he's far down the list as he's not an emergency, they say.

Gracias. He is to me.

*   *   *

Let's to the pub, Lethal. Perchance to drink a half. The night is young. The ale beckoneth. I wear my new jeans and Lacostes. Chilly evening but there is winter sun on the fields, shadows closing, slow

107

birds making last-minute loops. I walk past my old school. Buenos tardes. Never taught me nothing here. Zero. Not even Spanish. Had to buy a CD for that. I give it the finger. Everyone speaks that one.

Usuals, as per. Someone has placed a sombrero on the bear's head. The bespattered painters and decorators are at the bar. Raven is pigeon-toed in his tight black jeans and leather jacket.

Good evetide, maestro. How goes it? He has notes in his wallet, a few twenties. He is a happy swag. We sit beside the roaring bear, as per.

Cheers, then. Rave's glass meets mine. His leather creaks.

To all who sail.

Me and him lean back, partake of, enjoy. We are in pensive mode, as befits.

I notice Rave's jacket is a size too small, it prevents him raising his glass all the way up to his lips, he has to dip like a bird. His hair is ink-black, combed into five stiff cones. Still got his vanity. A whiff of hairspray makes me cough. Rave inspects his beer.

Did you know that yeast has got its own genetic code? he says. They say more than likely it's been put on earth by highly evolved alien life forms for investigative purposes. True fact, Lee.

I nod. Yeah? Cool. How's work?

Bedlam.

Bedlam is not a word I've heard him use before.

We are ants, Lee. Mere ants. Living on a giant anthill. The ultimate experiment.

Seems that way sometimes, I say.

That's because it's a fact. Think about it. An ant doesn't know he's an ant, does he? Rave creaks as he leans back. He raises his eyebrows.

Reckon I might travel, I say.

Set sail pronto, shipmate. Save a berth for me, he says. Cheers.

I'm not sure Raven has ever been abroad. We had a plan four years ago to drive across America. We had a route. We started saving. I was at Viking Direct in those days on the Brimsdown Estate. We had T-shirts printed, *Rave & Lee Coast 2 Coast— Are you ready USA?* It wasn't meant to rhyme. Rave's mum got them done at Snappy Snaps. I've never worn mine, it's the thought that counts. We still haven't finalised a date yet but it won't be this year.

Australia has been on my mind, I say.

The water goes down the wrong way, says Rave.

Reckon I could do well there. Bigger place, I say, fewer people, speak the lingo.

G'day, mate, says Rave.

But. Can't see Ned adapting.

Gud onya, Lethal. Might join you.

We sup our beer.

I don't answer.

I see my funeral cortège in a dream, making its way up Rowntree Road. Halting the traffic, causing obstruction. Policemen line the road. Leading the mourners are Lorelle and Caitlin, arm in arm, dressed to the nines. They seem equally distraught, fifty-fifty. Don't cry, I want to say. C'est la vie. Do not dwell. Buonasera señoritas. I cannot tell if Caitlin is wearing a leotard.

17

DRIER, CLEARER, WITH MORE MODERATE WINDS, WHICH WILL EASE LATER ON

It's different when it's one of your own, it would be. A blustery day. The sun dazzles when the clouds part, making us squint. Derek and his bearers have Lester on their shoulders. Derek looks the job in his finery, scrubs up well, always did. Coffin looks a treat, considering, handles glinting in the sunshine. From here you would never guess they are plastic rather than actual brass.

Organ music. I didn't order that, it just comes with. A bit like a car alarm going off, you have to wait till it's over. We follow on. I have never seen Ned in a suit. I loaned him one of mine, too big of course. His hair is wet-combed, centre parting. He looks like one of those homeless kids in the ads, Please help . . . His head twists left and right, taking it all in. Derek and his bearers step slow, steady on the red carpet. Lester glides aloft on the shoulders of working men. A decent send-off. He couldn't complain.

He is laid on the catafalque. The bearers step back. A pause. The bearers bow to the coffin. They straighten up. Precise. Clockwork. They depart, eyes down, hands clasped. Short of a six-gun salute Lester could not have had it more dignified.

I am the resurrection and the life, saith the Lord.

The vicar is a small man with a big voice. He does most of ours. Derek reckons he could have gone on the stage had he not been called by God.

He that believeth in me, though he were dead, yet shall he live, and whosoever liveth and believeth in me shall never die.

We do not sing a hymn. There's only three of us, including Lester's half-sister from Braintree, who we've never met. They suggested a CD. I said no. I don't reckon it's fair to Ned. We have a minute's silence instead.

The Lord is my Shepherd, I shall not want. He maketh me to lie down in green pastures; he leadeth me beside the still waters.

Three voices mumble. Ned stares at the coffin.

The vicar steps forward, spreads his arms. I am seized by an image of Les singing *What's New Pussycat?*

Let us commend Lester John Palmer to the mercy of God, our Maker and Redeemer.

Ned sniffs, gasps. I am surprised. I place my hand on his shoulder. Leave your hand too long you have intruded, too short and it is offhand. A relative should feel secure, unhurried. Remember, Lee, you are not Dracula.

Earth to earth, ashes to ashes, dust to dust. Same old. In the sure and certain hope, or uncertain hopeless sure-enough. We are miracle workers, Lee. Nobody cares if God is infinite or indefinite. Fetch me a magic wand.

I give Nate my arm as we file out. As we go I hear Lester, clear as day: The blind leading the blind. Love it.

*   *   *

I do not have a problem being chef in this house. Ned always cleans his plate, which I take as a

111

compliment. There are many decent cider recipes, not all of them pork. I am considering getting up earlier and having me another rabbit. Two in the pot will make enough casserole to freeze. If you're an early riser, you don't need a ferret. I have seen them evenings near the woods. Those very same bandoleros will likewise be around at dawn. Buenos noches, amigos.

It's all about mindset. We don't do innards at work—I was unprepared. I can prep a bunny if I'm in the right frame of mind. Second time around, third time lucky. A decent saving on meat. No probs. I shall merely step out at dawn with my weapon and my narrow eye. Hasta la vista, baby.

Sky is heavy, wind in the trees. I slam the door by way of letting Ned know I am not in. They say no two skies are ever the same. Same goes for a snowflake or a prang on the dual carriageway. A shame then to waste this sky. I pause at the mast. A smell of metal in the air.

I check the lane. People don't walk this route these days. I keep an eye out nevertheless. Two people questioned, apparently, no one arrested. Can't be too careful. Stalkers, chasers. I'm ready. If I had the .22 I'd give him a scare, nick him in the leg, the arm. That's a warning for you, my friend.

18

EARLY RAIN AND BRISK WINDS WILL EASE QUICKLY AND MOVE EASTWARDS LATER ON

It's funny what you get used to. I would not have touched a Healthy Options Prawn Salad the first month I worked here and now I look forward to it.

I have hoovered both Relatives Rooms. I start on Chapel 1. We're not allowed to hoover if a coffined client is waiting to be viewed, though it's OK to dust. Even when empty it feels all wrong to hoover the chapels, not that they're especially holy, what with the Axminster tufted and the air chillers on. I can't put my finger on it. The dead deserve some peace and quiet. Important to respect their needs, it's not like they want much. Dead men need no one and nothing. Fair play to them, we could all take a tip. I learned it off them: need nothing, be patient.

Lorelle pops by at lunchtime. I make a dash for the loo: hair, breath, spinach.

All right, Lee?

Well, hello. Wasn't expecting you.

I can't stop. Just dropping the ones for the four o'clock.

You can't resist my tea, though. Don't try to fight it, I say, suddenly inspired.

She rolls her eyes.

I like it when Lorelle leans against the wall while I brew up in the office, like we're in our own kitchen. We're not, of course. Irene is there frowning at her screen, mouthing words. She pretends not to listen but she does. I want to mention my poem but something stops me.

Ever been to Turkey? Lorelle asks.

Not Turkey, no, I say.

Nor me, she says. I quite fancy it.

Turkey's nice, says Irene, without looking up from her screen.

A moment. Me and Lorelle look at each other. I stir the teas. Lorelle smiles when I pass hers. I always offer the handle. I burn myself but I careth not.

I went to Paris on the train, May Bank Holiday, two years ago, Lorelle says.

Irene starts to hum. Not a tune, just arbitrary notes, any old. Just to cover up that she's listening. Impossible to be yourself when someone's having a nose. Especially when they're pretending not to. Especially when you're making the moves on a drop-dead gorgeous florist. I try to relax. I lean on Howard's empty desk.

Ever had artichoke hearts? I ask. I speak casual, at a level I hope Irene won't hear.

Lorelle blinks. What?

I would definitely recommend that particular dish if you are ever in the vicinity of Il Terrazzo, I say.

Derek spins in.

There you are! I'll be burying myself at this rate. What the eff are you doing? Pardon my French, Lauren.

I collect the cups. Derek never remembers Lorelle's name. Irene hums three loud notes and turns the printer on.

One of these days I will hold open the door of the van and lean in to kiss Lorelle as she clicks on

114

her seat belt. On the nose, on the cheek. Nothing too forward. Circling my prey. But not today. I am waylaid again by Derek who, as it turns out, only wants to mention that the rocket leaves in his ciabatta taste like pissed-on dandelions. The delay means that Lorelle has already slammed the door before I get there. Timing. Spoilt opportunity, but. I'm a great believer in fate. Fate will find a way. I wave to the back of the van as it disappears up Seddlescombe Road.

*   *   *

I boil up for the teas and coffees, arrange the mugs on the tray. Some people expect us to be religious here. We can be if required, it's not a problem, we have crucifixes at the ready. Many of our deceased clients wear a religious symbol in their coffin, even if they didn't in life.

Relatives like a little bit of something godly when they're on the premises. Almost everyone wants prayers and Bible readings at the funeral service, as befits. I saw a family member cross himself with his mobile phone last week. God is in the modern world, moving mysteriously. He is probably on YouTube.

All denominations and believers are welcome here, even if we do not partake ourselves. Saying that, Mikey has leanings. He believes in God but he doesn't go to church. There's someone watching over us, he says, but he can't be more specific than that.

Irene is the most religious here, even though she writes a stern letter when a payment is late. She goes to church Christmas, Lent and Easter. She will always lend you a fiver but she wants it back.

Howard is on the fence. He likes Christianity, the hymns, the palaver, but. He can't say if there's a God or not and he won't be drawn. He said he admires Sufis. That shut us up. Derek does not believe. He says he did as a boy but the Royal Navy put paid to it. He may have drifted back to the fold, he says, but working with the deceased has warped his point of view. For me I would like to think there is a God, but it doesn't look good from here. We don't get bogged down, to be honest. We deal with the here and now. Paperwork, paperwork. We have to get them in their coffins, get them sorted, checked, checked again. Me and Derek need the odd little joke to get us through the day. Caution is the byword, mind you. Derek always says that. Once your reputation's gone in this game, you're dead, he says. Always the joker, but keep it behind closed doors. A good rep is important around the living but it's one hundred per cent critical around the deceased.

19

A FINE DAY, SUNNY AT FIRST WITH LIGHT SHOWERS
DEVELOPING IN THE SOUTH-WEST

He comes out of thin air. He loves it when I flinch. He lets out one of his giant elf laughs. I hear him breathing, thinking. I hear him moving, beads raining. He rests on the table, tipping it, blowing through his mouth, calculating my reaction. He smells of popcorn and BO. The hairs on his legs look blond under the desk lamp. Where Ned's overall blondness went I cannot say, lost in the past with whatever it was we used to be.

He is semi-dressed, my clothes mainly. Upside-down words are written in black pen on his arm. He knocks my paperwork to the floor: electric bill, BT, estate agent correspondence. His hands sign.

Gog. Very bad headache. Bad. Bad. Medicine now.

He peers sleepily through his hair. How come his skin looks good when he barely washes?

He does this, interrupts. What he needs. More important, always was.

I don't sign, I speak.

Hold your horses.

Ow, he signs again. Ow me. Head. Bad, bad.

Doing it, aren't I? I shout. I sound upset.

Ow! Ow! Ow! He pulls my arm.

I close my eyes. Drives you round. Literally drives you.

Keep your hair on, I tell him.

He gasps. He thumps me on the shoulder. I turn to look at him. What in fuck's name? I shove him in the chest. He runs to shove me back but I move first. I push him all the way till we hit the wall together. I leave him there.

I stroll to the cupboard, take out the aspirin bottle. Child lock. Three goes it takes to unscrew the lid. Camel's back anyone? For *fucks*! It gives. Finally. Ned watches, blowing through his mouth. I chuck the lid. Then because I can't stop, because I'd like to strangle him, squeeze his throat until. I shake out the pills all over the floor.

We stand and watch while they skitter in all directions, hundreds of them running for freedom. As the last one settles I lob the empty bottle into the air, a final gesture, pointless. I giveth not. It bounces off the draining board, lands in the washing-up bowl. Olé, arsehole. Ned watches with suspicious interest, like when he's watching Sky News. One or two tablets are crushed under my shoes as I go. I slam the door the way she used to; it bounces open behind me.

He never heard a single door she ever slammed, I heard every one. Some things he will never know. I leave him there surrounded by enough cut-price aspirin to top himself before tea if he's lucky, do us all a favour. Buenos noches, Knobflap.

I fetch my key. I let the back door slam. He will feel it. I am making a point. He knows full well where the aspirin is, how to switch on the hot water immersion, but he won't do it.

Lee does it three hundred and sixty-five, no time off for good behaviour. But Ned is the genius, the superstar. Why doesn't he do it? Why me? No point carping. C'est la vie, Lee. No one hears. No one answers. I hear enough for two. No big deal, just outlining the facts.

*   *   *

I've started to read Lorelle like a book. Body language. Say what you like but your body says it better. Bodies tell the truth. As a matter of fact, due to this knowledge, I know I'm in with a chance. Result.

The giveaways are (1) Neck and throat exposure and (2) Hair-swinging. If she touches her hair, neck or throat you're done and dusted. Game on. Which is how I know I'm on the grid. I know what you're thinking, but. There is nothing Lorelle could deduce from my body language that would give her a clue as to how I feel. The reason being that I am body-aware. For example, I adopt a neutral stance: feet apart, hands in pockets, noncommittal eye contact. I don't move a muscle, I do not touch my hair. I look ahead, give nothing away. Granted, I smile, but I keep it short and sweet. Women don't like to see a man expressing himself, it puts them off. If you want to get their attention, stealth is the word.

You're not supposed to understand them, Lee, they're made different. Ready? *Lift*.

Mr Parker is a big man. Takes two of us to move him. Four of us would be easier. We have to bend our knees.

One two three.

We catch our breath. Derek's not one for body language.

Ne'er the twain, says Derek. Many before have

tried to read a woman and failed, he adds.

One two three.

We are halfway between the drawer and the table. A rock and a hard place, Derek says. We stop to catch our breath again.

You'll never get the gist of a woman, Lee. They are leagues ahead. See us coming, son. Just when you think you've got the measure, they pull a swift one. They can't help it, nature of the beast. Stand up for yourself, never fails.

Derek is panting with all the talking and lifting. He pauses. It occurs to me what a right knob anyone would feel dropping dead trying to shift a cadaver. I keep that thought to myself. I count us in instead.

Uno dos tres.

Mr Parker is on the trolley. We high-five. We bend over our knees. On the trolley Mr Parker will have to stay, it is the manual hydraulic hoist type for ease of height adjustment.

Derek gasps. The armpits of his shirt are wet.

Get that kettle on, he says, before one of us drops.

With that, one of Mr Parker's arms swings off the trolley. Timing. The dead have it in spades, same as the living.

Today when I woke my first thought was Lorelle. Don't get me wrong, Caitlin is a lovely girl, but. Lorelle Connelly you've got me on my knees. I thought about popping into Fleurtations. I could say I found myself in the vicinity, something like that. I decide to do so from the comfort of my own bed. A private encounter, the kind that rarely goes wrong when it's just you and your imaginings. Live it in your own head. Result. And wouldn't you just know it, she's on her own minding the shop, while the others do deliveries.

Buongiorno.

We start off polite.

How's it going? Not too bad, yourself? What you been up to? This and that and you? The same. Usual, as per.

After which it's time to kiss her.

Oh my God, Lee.

Come here, I say.

She wraps her arms around my neck. Passionately.

Oh Lee, she says.

I bend her backwards over the ferns. We peel off our shirts without breaking the kiss. You thought only movie stars could do that. Wrong. She angles sharply for a second kiss, tipping dangerously. A tub of roses goes over. I catch her before she topples. The phone rings. Knobs to that. I stub my toe on a tin bath but not before I clear the desk in one swipe: stapler, cards, wrapping, the lot: on the deck. You thought only movie stars could do that. Wrong again. She laughs. I lift her on to the desk. She pulls me towards her. I balance on my knees, support her waist. The desk bumps the shelves which wobble the display which hits the selection of terracotta pots which knock the filigree ironwork, making everything go ding ding ding. I lift her off the desk. We land against the storeroom door, which we slam: tres, cuatro, cinco. Until it shuts.

Lorelle is wearing me out and we haven't even gone on a date yet. I haven't asked her. I will. I don't want to frighten her off. Timing. Stealth. Artichoke hearts. One hundred squids. A bit like waiting for rabbit with the .22, no good rushing in waving it about. Patience. Dead men teach it best.

20

A FINE AND DRY DAY WITH A GOOD DEAL OF SUNSHINE
AND SOME LIGHT WINDS

I was close, easy angle. Still. I got lucky. One shot.
It is lying in the leaves with its fingers curled under
its chin. I pick it up and it flops, warm, in my hand.
Just behind the ear; the brightest blood I have seen,
sticky to the touch. I am a hunter. I walk. I carry my
squirrel. Everything seems pin-clear. Even the grass
shines.

I walk up to the ruined barn. That's what Mum
called it, as if someone had gone and spoiled it. It's
not so much ruined as dilapidated, but we're not
the sort of family to say dilapidated. It's got three
sides and half a roof, rusted bits of machinery, torn
plastic sheeting inside. You could do something
with it if you had a mind to. Lester said that before
his mind went askew. Personally I like it as it is.
Where the wood has dropped away you can see
rectangles of sky or trees. You get the impression
creatures come at night to roost or think, whatever.
It's not indoors or outdoors, but a bit of both, best
of both worlds. It's got a sense of oldness, like it
knows something you don't and it's watching to see
if you catch on.

I stand on the bridge over the flyover with my
squirrel. Not a bad sunset. Streaks of red-pink
in layers on the horizon. Below is the commuter
traffic. Flash vehicles, company cars. Knobheads. I
wave the squirrel at them. One of them looks up.

It was not my idea to place a dual carriageway here. If I'm sitting on the fence and some driver stares at me, I think, It's not me who shouldn't be here, it's you.

I watch the crows settling to roost. Craak, craak. Restless they are this time of day; one lifts and off they all go in a raggy circle before settling again. Everything looks good under a pink sky, even the flyover. I wait for Crow, he knows me.

Evening, Lee. On your own again?

There is an oak fence before you get to the woods, then it runs to barbed wire. I always sit on the same fence. If Crow doesn't appear I mosey up to the woods. He likes to play hard to get. I don't blame him. If I had wings you wouldn't see which way I went.

I will check the lane and surrounding area but I have given up hope of intercepting any unsavoury A-level-student-chasing character hereabouts. A pity. Reckon I could've done the world a favour there. He won't chance his arm again. Not with me on the prowl.

Green burials are becoming increasingly popular, I hear. We don't offer woodland burial; we should. Unconsecrated ground doesn't bother people the way it did. We never went to church, she preferred the idea of Buddhism, she liked the colours.

With woodland burial you're allowed to mark the spot with a tree, no stones or memorials. Job done. Anyway, you can get tired of HERE LIES and RIP, talk about unimaginative.

The official line at Shakespeare's is one of scepticism, but. You can't afford to be too sceptical in the funeral trade. For this reason we do offer a wicker coffin and, as of recently we have added the cardboard coffin to the menu. Biodegradable is very in. We offer it with an oak-effect shell casement, so your loved-one doesn't resemble a delivery from Ikea. Alternatively you can plump for one of the decorated ones, Union Jack being quite popular, along with Division One teams. Man U is the bestseller, according to the distributor, Cloud Visions UK. Doesn't have to be Premier League.

Around here it's hard to get the ball rolling. This is not London or Brighton. The oldies are not keen. The words bio and degrade mean something else to the over-sixties, Derek pointed out. Never occurred to me. He's a lot more switched-on than you think.

I prepare my frying pan. I have never cooked squirrel. I decide to approach it as I would chicken. I check it out on eHow. For this I enter Ned's room alone, while he watches *Property Ladder* downstairs. I brave the dirty underwear, the stink, the half-eaten food, the welcoming wall of naked bodies, *Buongiorno, ladies*, and the unexpected; like Mum's old flip flops and the fish slice Ned uses to scratch his back. I collect the dirty plates on my way out.

I know what to do. I wash the blood off its head and dry the squirrel with the tea towel. It looks nice. I could have it stuffed. For a minute I can't decide. Eeny-meeny. I lay it in the sink. It's all about mindset. Come on, Lee. I am not squeamish, but. It is necessary to chop off its hands and feet. Then peel off its fur. This is rabbit revisited. Been here, done it—this time is different. Needs must.

I lay the squirrel on the breadboard. I position the knife. Uno dos tres. Fuck. Call yourself a hunter? I can't do it. Something about the hands and feet. I open the freezer. I lay the squirrel in beside the rabbit. This is bollocks. Beatrix knobbing Potter on ice.

Ned is sunbathing on a small towel outside. He wears boxers, mine, and sunglasses, hers. He doesn't seem to notice the gusts of wind. I was going along the lines of a fricassee but now I reckon I'll do vegetarian instead. I get out the .22 to reload. I step outside to feel the sun on my neck. The sky is empty except for some straggly birds. The sun dings off the trampoline frame. I check the scope, aim.
    Ned.
    I fire into the grass beside him. A flick of earth. After a moment he raises his head, stares at the sky, then rests it down again. I go indoors. I put the water on to boil for dinner. I would never hurt him, as if.

21

DRY OVERNIGHT WITH LONG CLEAR SPELLS. MIST AND FOG PATCHES WILL FORM IN PLACES

Ned is on the trampoline. He is attempting to take a photo of himself on his phone in mid-air. I could probably get him sectioned for that. Not that I would, obviously.

I put the kettle on. Ned has forty-seven friends on Facebook. Out of those he has met eight in person: Raven, Nell, Jock and Dianne from the kennels, Eileen from the medical centre, Mr Gupta's son from the Tesco Express Garage, our fifteen-year-old cousin Corrine from Margate, and me. I don't bother with it these days. You grow out of it, I reckon. Ned posts images of himself on his personal page, mainly wearing disguise. Ned in hats, Ned in sunglasses, Ned pouting like a fish. There's one of him laughing. At what?

When my mourning rig went missing I had my suspicions. Denies it, well he would. Following day there it is on Facebook for all to gander, top hat too big of course. One of his eyes blown up giant through our mum's old magnifying glass. I did not give permission for that. It's easy to mock, but. Death is a skilled business. Important to get it right. People depend on it to mend their grief. A dead man's dignity comes from the slow hearse, the polished handles, the top hat and tails. No one is ready. Not me, not even Derek. Especially not Derek. Everyone is immortal till they're not.

Who will prepare the deceased when Derek is

gone? You might think Dereks are ten a penny, ditto Howards. I for one would rather be dead with Derek than alive with some people. Only joking, but I know what I mean.

Spaghetti we'll have with grated cheese. I turn on the tap, fill the pot.

Derek says you grow accustomed to the job one body at a time. I wouldn't disagree. People are people, alive or dead, some speak to you more than others, simple as. I wait for the water to boil. I take a load off in the chair.

You won't last a week. So sayeth Lester when I got the job at Shakespeare's. I don't blame him, most people wouldn't last. I didn't think I'd last. Same with trawler fishing apparently, a lot of people just can't take it. You could call it a vocation more than a job, I like that. I was only after a job and I ended up with a career. Nice one. It only has one drawback after all, not that it bothered me for long. Within the week I was talking to dead men and thinking, I know living people less interesting than these. And that's when I knew. Now I look forward to coming to work. Once all the jokes about a dead-end job were out of the way I realised, in fact, I had it made in the shade.

I lay the table. Set our giraffe salt and pepper grinders at the centre. We bought them for Mum's fortieth birthday. All these years and we still can't tell which is the salt giraffe and which is pepper.

Lester used to have his dinner on a tray in those days so he could watch *Come Dine With Me* or *Wife Swap*. His excuse was he'd run out of dinner conversation. As if Ned and me were brimful, like mini Oscar Wildes. Our mother loved Oscar

Wilde—right up her street, the artier-fartier the better. Far as she was concerned arty-farty was the be-all and end-all, thank you and goodnight. Meanwhile I am left at the table with Ned for a dining companion. He's got zero etiquette, he eats noisy. This is how she must have felt, trying to keep everything decent and à la mode. Trying to stick it all together with organic chutney and napkins, whereas I decided long ago just to use paper serviettes.

*   *   *

She got worse. Les brought her downstairs to lie on the settee, where she could look at the view of the field and woods.

She sent off for personalised affirmations prepared by a guru who lived just off the A40. He sent her a pamphlet: *Destabilisation occurs when the energy fields of your body are incorrect.* The pamphlet went on to explain this had been proved beyond all doubt in the 1950s by a Russian. After the correct treatment patients awoke to find their tumours had disappeared overnight. She affirmed. She smiled. She connected to her Higher Power. Someone in America was found online who could cure her from across the Atlantic. They needed her blood type and her astrological sign. They could cure her long distance for only two hundred dollars. She knew she was blood type A. The American emailed to tell her blood type A meant she was a co-operative, sensitive, passionate, self-controlled person. That's accurate, she said. We admitted it was uncanny. We crossed fingers. We touched wood. We threw salt. Anything was possible. You just had to believe.

22

PATCHY LIGHT RAIN POSSIBLE INITIALLY, OTHERWISE DRY WITH SOME SUNSHINE AT TIMES

Newsflash. Shakespeare's is to be taken over by Greenacre Funeralcare Group PLC. Like a sardine swallowed by a whale there is nothing we can do. Greenacre have their own way of doing things, a system. It is not the same as our system. There are no nylon picnic chairs, no running gags or jokes biro'd on the wall; no end-of-line Hot Sensation lipsticks, no Tupperware or radios. Moreover, they are very efficient, apparently.

A single manager runs several outlets at once, travelling between them in his company Mazda, co-ordinating, overseeing. They have a floating embalmer, I am told. Ditto hearse and coffin personnel. They can remove, interview, prep, coffin and bury all at the same time, we hear. This is due to their system. They have back-up and spreadsheets. They can despatch their experts hither and yon. So sayeth our man on the ground, aka Howard. You only have to look at Howard to see he is not expecting to be hired by Greenacre. The expression on his face reminds me of Roy Hodgson when Blackpool beat Liverpool at Anfield. Wan is the word.

Derek took the news on the chin at first, but lately he's gone downhill. He is heading for the abyss, Irene said. She has known Derek a long time. I am shocked at her use of the word abyss.

A cloud has settled over Shakespeare & Son.

Gone are random chats, wit and banter, things are no longer off the cuff. Death is a serious business when it's a way of life. Fair to say some of us have lost the spring in our step. If clients were able to complain they might well object to a general lack of staff congeniality on the job. Guilty as charged. Not a leg to stand on.

We have been reassured that each of us will be considered for employment by Greenacre, to which Derek answered, Do they think we were born yesterday? To which the Greenacre rep did not reply. The silence made everyone blink.

We are not fools, Howard says, after the rep has gone. We know where we stand, he says. We have begun to walk and talk like actors in a spaghetti western. We know exactly where we stand—in the past. Life has changed. So has death. We are the future unemployed and we know it. C'est la vie.

When tea is ready I bang the handle of the long mop on the ceiling. Ned feels the vibration and comes down. I stand for a moment to take in all the mop bang marks on the ceiling from other teas Ned has come down for. I wonder how many teas we have had, in total. Maybe one day tour parties will stand on this very spot. Like the Pyramids, this house will stand as a monument. Yes, and the tour guide will say, If you look directly up you can in fact see the marks on the ceiling made by the young Lee Hart as he beckoned his deaf brother down for tea. He won't come down of course. Not till it's cold.

She picked him to love most because he was the weak one. I don't blame her, women have a soft spot for the runt. Our mum was a bedazzled woman but Ned threw it all away. Who knows why?

No point asking. Being deaf was not the problem. Being deaf was his brilliance, his proudest moment. He lost his flair after she died. I knew he'd flake, she didn't.

These days I am happier at work. The living and the dead get along famously. Job done. Clear cut as. Currently we are riding a wave of optimism due to a rumour that suggests we will all be retained by Greenacre at this outlet for the time being. Nothing to fret about. No ghosts, none, they all live at home.

*   *   *

Mrs Delaney's daughter has arranged for her mother to be buried with her mobile phone switched on. Everyone gathers in the office to discuss it. This is something new for Shakespeare's. I abandon the boiling kettle to join the debate. We speak over each other.

It's good to talk, says Derek. Everyone laughs. He got that off the BT ad. Nice.

Connecting people, I say. Like off the Nokia ad. No one seems to know that one. I say it again. I have boiled the kettle three times now due to the excitement.

Howard, on the other hand, takes his time, speaks slowly, smiles serenely, as if he buries ringing phones with clients every single week. I thought everyone knew the Nokia ad.

Me personally, the last thing I'd want in my coffin is the phone going off. *Rest In Peace* it says on her plate, talk about mixed messages. I've never myself heard of a phone actually going off, though now and then you'll hear it on the grapevine.

Nice family. They all walk the same, head pitched forward, like a family of egrets. Mrs Angelou, the daughter, talks softly, dips her head to listen. It's infectious. Now we're all doing it, creeping about whispering, dipping, bobbing. Even Derek. Spread like wildfire. Mental. Howard and Derek in particular are under Mrs Angelou's spell. I am hanging back in the shadows, the corridors are congested as it is.

The only time Derek took longer over a prep was with the fiancé policeman, who drowned himself last year after getting dumped on his wedding eve.

True, Mrs Angelou is a looker. Irene put her finger on it. There at her desk, she bursts out: You men are so predictable!

There is no answer to that. Irene is right. In spite of this or maybe because of it, me, Derek and Howard categorically deny it there and then: We're not all alike you know. Tarred with the same brush. One bad apple doesn't spoil the whole bunch.

Irene is silenced. No one said life was fair, only short.

Derek has gone all out on Mrs Delaney, the mother. I took a peek on my return from a two o'clocker. Smart. All in black, hands clasped, rosary draped. Derek has covered his tracks. Plenty of stuffing at the elbows and her hands have come together, natural as. A bit of smoke and mirrors. No other way, dead hands don't clasp.

A picture, I say to Derek.

I thang you.

Busy with the cheek pads? I say.

He puts his hands on his hips, turns in his knee, like he might dance.

Anything else? he asks.

133

I take a look. Colour in her cheeks. Sheen on her hair. Lipstick: Blushing Bride I'd hazard. Skin tone. Eye sockets. We step back for a moment to take her all in. There's trickery here, but nothing unusual leaps out. Whatever he's done he's done well.

What, no telling? I say.

Nothing to tell, he says. If you can't see it it ain't there. He winks. Know what I mean, Lee?

Mrs Angelou will dip her head and thank Derek in her softly softly voice and Derek will dip his head in return and take her hand and look in her eyes, but his lips will remain sealed.

I write down the personal effects in the big book: Leather Bible, St Joseph Daily Prayer Book, an image of the Holy Virgin, three photographic portraits and a Motorola V6. Charged.

I've got a Samsung, but not the Galaxy S. Without Ned I'd have an iPhone by now. No point craving what you haven't got.

When Mrs Delaney is finally laid to rest, there will doubtless be a chirrup below ground to wake her. The electronic words will lie with Mrs Delaney until the end of time. Or at least till the battery goes. God keep you. We love you. We are with you, now and always.

I'm no philosopher but. Some things show their colours no matter what. I stand on the landing, taking in the moonlight on the field: clouds parted, crop shining—like Jesus might stroll on and speak—tell me what to do, like he does in his films.

Jesus, how long till (a) I get a table for two at Il Terrazzo? (b) A position at Greenacre? (c) A life without my brother? He wouldn't answer of course.

More important things than.

In my game you wonder what will it say on your stone when you cop it. Whether you will get flowers, what they will say. I hope I get Lorelle's writing on the card: *You crack me up, Lee. He he. Gotta rush. R.I.P.* I don't stand there dwelling long.

I missed her yesterday, we were at a burial up the B2036. Second time this week I missed her. I find my phone.

Hav u hurd we r 4 the chop? c'est la vie. how r u? Lee.

I press send.

*   *   *

Not that I'm religious but, if I was going to pray, I'd pray for Howard's job. Reckon I'd be handy. Watch and learn, that's me. When Lorelle is Mrs Hart we will run it together, two Harts are better than one. That's my trajectory, career-wise. I've got nothing against Howard, obviously, but it's dog eat dog in this world.

SOME LOW CLOUD AND MISTINESS, TURNING FOGGY
LATER WITH DRIZZLE POSSIBLE

Ned is watching *Dancing on Ice: The Dance Off*. He is chewing monkey nuts and dropping the shells where they fall. His foot is on the coffee table, inserted inside a bag of frozen sweetcorn. The night before last I returned from the pub to discover, in my absence, he had conducted an impromptu experiment that involved seeing how close his ski socks could get to the fire before they caught alight. Now he knows. Cheers, Ned. Home insurance policy anyone? Only one sock caught before the experiment was declared officially over.

You knob. I sign.

Knobs is us, he signs.

Mess, I sign him. Look.

Fuck you, thank you. He signs back, smiling.

Mess. You make pig. Clean.

He scoops a handful of shells and flings them in my direction. They roll and scatter; one bounces off my shoe.

Very good, Gog. Hoover Hoover.

Don't get me wrong, I have a sense of humour same as the next man, but. He pushes his. He push push fucking pushes.

I thump him hard on the side of the head. He yells, thrashes.

Shells, nuts, ice, sweetcorn. Arrivederci todos. He's on his feet. He throws his fists, one after the other, while I jag to the side. He misses, misses,

misses.

Ha! Arsehole! Come on! Here we are at last, communicating. Come on! I sign. Come on! He comes. Lunging, flailing. I duck away, stamping shells, nuts, sweetcorn. I am quick as. I run rings round him. Where'd I go?

Missed!

I attack from behind. Wallop. Buenos dias!

He's angry now. Gets me back with a chop to my arm. For *fucks*.

I grab his shirt, drag him across the room. We stagger, thumping, blocking, swinging. I land another: a mighty smack on the gob, a wild one. Knuckles on teeth. Crack. He goes down.

The pain hammers me into the floor. I double up. One knobhead, two knobhead, three. I reckon I might kick him as he lies there. I do. Free kick from the corner. Whap. He is silent, aka a foul. Penalty kick from the box. Don't mind if I do. I swing a belter into his thigh.

There it is. Thin at first. Boo-hoo. A little girl's noise. Little Bo Baa has lost her sheep. Sniff sniff. Same old. Same old. I slam the back door.

He is not of this world, never was. Touched by genius, she said. Trouble is some div's got to clean up after. Same old div, as per. I am at the mast in seconds. I don't stop. Glad there is a wind to walk against, it takes my breath away. Gracias. Walking walking. Where to? Nowhere, that's where. Around in circles. Day after day after.

It was Ned who sprayed Lee Hart is a knobhead on the inside of the bus shelter. Cheers. He still thinks I don't know. I didn't at first. Never thought he had the initiative. Not just the bus shelter: a parking bay at the library, the wall by the Coinwash and a skip opposite the Somerfield car park. He carried on till he'd used up a whole can of blue paint.

Not everyone could handle it. Lucky I am the sort of person who can turn the other cheek.

When he tips backwards through his bedroom window, he's only thinking of the buzz, like a kid. Not to begrudge him, I'm just saying. The trampoline always catches him, but one day. And whose fault will that be? Everything changes in the spring. It always does.

There is a note on the draining board.

Gog. How goes? Potatoes in the oven. Yum. Cheers! Ned.

I turn slowly, half expecting to find him on the ceiling. What's he up to? What the. All the dishes are put away. The floor is clean. I move quickly through and find the lounge is tidy, spotless, Hoovered.

Ned?

I run upstairs. What the hell is going. The bedrooms are empty. I try the bathroom. He is lying in a full bath, no bubbles, one sponge.

Ned?

I wait. For whatever. Blood, electricity, monkey nuts. His hands come up talking from under the water.

Gog! How goes? Hungry? One minute. OK?

Drip drip drip.

I wait nervously downstairs. I try to think who he might have insulted, bothered, murdered. Whether the police have been round. What is missing, stolen, sold? Think. A clink of ice. I turn. Ned offers a tumbler of Lester's old Jameson's with ice. Service with a smile.

I take it.

Ta, his hand reminds me.

Ta, I sign. Cheers, mate.

Cheers! he signs. He breathes through his mouth, strolls across the rug, hands on his hips. I scan for more clues. His hair is combed into straight wet sections, his ears poke out. His skin, teeth, appear to be clean. Unusual. He looks carefully at me, winks, nods. What the. Drink drink, he signs. I wonder if it's poisoned.

Good days, he signs.

Good days. Yeah.

Hungry?

He sprints for the kitchen. Something is seriously.

He lunges back in.

Welcome! Food is ready, he signs.

We eat together at the table. Nothing is wrong that I can tell, not yet, maybe not at all. He slurps, smacks, burps, as per. Grins at me. He touches my arm.

Why can't it always be like this? he signs.

After dinner we watch the ten o'clock news. He is watching it for my sake. He'd rather watch *Britain's Next Top Model* or *Tool Academy*, something with pretty girls.

Nighty night night, he signs at the end and disappears to bed.

Something is seriously up. I take the cushion, throw it in front of him. He turns.

What's all this? I sign.

What?

You dinner cook, tidy, clean, weird.

So? What?

139

Why?

Never mind what what what. Say thank you, Ned. Ta. He drops his hands.

Ta, Ned, I sign. Very nice.

Very welcome, Gog. Night night.

I have been sitting with her while the sun goes down on the field. I cannot tell if she is here. You are supposed to tell, I think, if they are around. I can't. I wait. I close my eyes. Nothing. I don't say her name, no point.

I walk back. The air is purple, a spot of pink over the flyover. I check my latest text.

v sorry 2 hear ur news re work. c u l8er. L.

I stroll, thinking on. About Lorelle, about the timing of my next move. She seems genuinely concerned. A chill in the ground, in the air. The birds have roosted.

A clack. I stop. Another. Clack. Something hits the fence post. Dack. A stone. Like a stone. Now I know what it is. I know exactly. Might've known. Should've seen it coming. I run towards the house. The light is gone but I know my way.

Clack. Something hits the ground beside me. I zag to the side.

I see him now. He is aiming through my bedroom window. He must've clocked me there a hundred times. The landing light is on, so he's backlit. Stupid arse. I see the .22 on his shoulder, his cheek on the stock, like he's falling asleep. I run for the back door.

We sit at the kitchen table waiting for the kettle to

140

boil. The .22 on the table. I'm not in the mood for a fight.

I slapped him and then I thought, that's it. I'm too tired.

Apologise you. Yes? Hello?

Very sorry, Gog. His hands drop, fold. The end.

I look at our reflection in the dark kitchen window. I see myself slumped. I see my head turn away, turn back to him.

You any thing say me? I sign.

Teach you me shoot?

The barrel of his finger points. His eyebrows are high. He looks hopeful. For fucks.

I get up to do the teas.

I don't think he meant to hurt me. Scare me, yes, show me he could. Nick me in the leg, maybe. He wanted to impress. I could be wrong, it has been known. I should be angrier, but.

24

DRY AND SUNNY, LIGHT NORTHWESTERLY WINDS MID-MORNING ONWARDS, CLOUDIER LATER

A clear, still day, greenery bursting, sunlight opening the early buds. The ground damp from the night's rain, a smell of fungus, woodsmoke. Quiet as. Just the clock going tick tock.

She doesn't die in my arms, as I'd imagined. She is restless for a while, then goes still. This is new. The lady who comes from the cancer charity has a word for it: Acceptance. She has a word for everything, or a pamphlet, or a list. We don't argue with her, we nod. We speak fluent pamphlet and leaflet. We take them politely, as if it will help. We listen, nod, agree, *accept*. We plod on, reading leaflets, boiling the kettle, waiting.

There are words and phrases that go with dying of cancer. According to the cancer charity lady there are five processes to complete during your dying: Forgiveness, Heartfelt Thanks, Sentiments of Love, Goodbye. None of us point out that's only four, because our mother doesn't bother with any of it, she hasn't read this pamphlet. Cancer charity lady encourages us to prompt Mum, but none of us can find the right cancer charity words. When her breathing gets loud, when I reach for her hand and she pulls away, cancer charity lady is on hand to explain that there is a word for this too: Separation. When her head tips back and she opens her mouth wide, I lean in because maybe she wants to speak. She doesn't. She wants to scream but has no sound.

She screams anyway, soundless, a silent movie. Only Ned hears it. The last thing to go is hearing, we are told. She can hear you right up to the end. Is it the end? We don't know. Is she dying? Cancer charity lady says she is. There is a word for it: Departure.

Ned kneels at her side like a person from a long time ago. I wonder if he can hear other things I cannot hear, silent things, just for him. She breathes in, stops. I breathe the out breath for her. Pick up where she left off. End of. Ned waits but I knew she was gone.

25

MAINLY DRY AND SUNNY. SOME MIST AND FOG
PATCHES WILL FORM IN PLACES, ESPECIALLY IN THE
SOUTH-WEST

Good evetides! I slap Rave's shoulder.
Sirrah! He slaps me back.
Best?
Please, mate.
He orders at the bar. Busy tonight. The paint-spattered decorators are on their stools. Still not quite dark outside but here, with all the lamps glowing, might as well be Christmas. The main crowd are not yet partying. Getting them in early we are, a nose in front. Plus we want to bags our usual table—best vantage point, see them coming all directions.
I check my hair in one of the pub brasses. I look like the minging Cheshire cat. I'm wearing my D&G shirt, my new jeans; feeling sharp. We're going on of course, after this. Not decided where, as yet. Probably Liaisons.
Lethal!
Raven has streaming pints at the ready.
Cheers, Ravester.
I carry them to our table. A song comes on and I have to break my stride so I don't look like I'm walking to the beat. One of them girl singers. No one to ask which song it is, just Ned at the table.
Cheers, I sign.
Cheers, Gog. Ta, he signs.
Raven joins.

Cheers. We raise.

Good evetides.

We raise to the grizzly.

All who sail.

The ale sinks, hits the spot. We relax, partake of. Raven's hairsprayed cones bob as he moves to the music. I check my hair. RokHard has done the job but my fringe has a habit of going curly when my back is turned. Ned doesn't have this problem, his hair shafts straight down either side of his brain, not a kink to be seen. He glances back at me. He looks normal in that shirt, another D&G, you'd never know he was such a div.

I thumb him. He thumbs-up back. Good boy.

Rave's got some coins. Quick gamble on the fruits, don't mind if I do. We leave Ned to guard the table.

Around about the time the big ladies arrive with their mini husbands, we're ready to roll on out of this joint.

Adios, amigos. Hasta luego. We return our glasses to the bar.

Cheers then, Keith.

Mind how you go.

We walk to the Rowntree Road. Chilly eve but dry. There are stars.

Look! I point them out. Millions looks like.

We stop by the playing fields to see if we can identify a constellation or two. Harder than you think. Constellations look easy on tea towels and mouse mats but they're complicated in the actual sky.

Shine down on me, cries Rave, spreading his arms. Ned spreads his arms too, walks in a circle. He laughs up at the sky, some kind of private joke between him and the universe.

I jump up, grab hold of the football goal; I try to swing, recapture my youth, perchance. I hang there under a million stars.

Could be the Big Dipper, says Rave, pointing up.

Then again, I say. Rave knows less than zero about constellations. You can't just make them up. My arms are killing. I drop to the ground. Nothing else here. We move on.

Ned won't let the stars drop. He trips over every kerbstone, gazing up, pointing, head in the clouds.

Come on! I have to wave to sign him.

Bit of a trek to Duke's Hill Road, longer in the dark.

Have we gone the wrong way, fellow Saracens? Rave wants to know. He lifts a cone of hair, looks around. We wait while Ned takes a wazz behind a Vauxhall Viva.

Finally. The bright lights. Buonasera. We cross at the Belisha beacon. Busy, even at this time. I bet my hair's gone curly. We stare at the neon sign. Rave says they've spelt *Liaisons* wrong. Too many i's? We can't decide. We careth not.

A rugby scrum at the bar. Rave is tallest because of his hair, but it's me who gets served in the end. Ned is enjoying himself. He can feel the beat through his bones, makes him grin. The lights are blue. They shine through glass pillars, even the bar is glass, like we've arrived at the North Pole.

No tables available. We line up against the wall with our drinks and take in the scenery. Too loud to talk. I notice Rave's drink has got leaves in it, mint I think. I ordered a cocktail too, apple martini. Ned's got a rum and Coke. Always gives him bad dreams, but you only live once.

I notice all three of us head-bobbing so I stop, three battery hens, for fucks. No one seems to have noticed. I scan for girls. A few in groups, some with boyfriends. They all look nice. A big cheer goes up in the corner and we turn. Everyone seems to know each other.

Imbibements? Rave shouts.

Why not? The eve is young.

Rave collects. Ned necks his rum and Coke, hands over his empty. Rave sets off into the crowd. We watch his uppermost hair cone travel like a fin through the sea of heads.

Ned burps.

Gog! How goes? he signs. He grins. A good situation, he signs. I thumbs-up. I nod. I feel like a knob to tell the truth. Don't know why. Too old for this place.

A white laser panics over our heads, looping the room and back again. Ned jumps up, applauds, points it out, tries to catch it.

We're at a table. We now have a camp, a base. We guard it. The music is louder but we don't bob. We sit heavy as rocks. We must concentrate, follow the laser, wait for it to illuminate a pretty girl. Maybe she will come to our base, sit with us. The laser is zagging about now. Too fast. No sooner do you see a pretty face before the thing skids off, lighting up bald patches, back of someone's throat, some bloke's arse. I stop watching it. I stare at the opposite wall instead.

Same again? Rave asks.

No mate. I'm all right.

Ned jerks out of his trance.

Please please, he signs. Extra ice. Ta, he signs.

I screen my mouth from Ned with my hand. No more rum! I shout at Rave.

I am alert, but motionless. A Komodo dragon. I am guarding the table. Every few minutes I have to shout: Yes, these seats are taken! People go on asking.

Ned is on the illuminated dance floor. He sidesteps around the perimeter of the square, waving his arms and peering into girls' faces. His smile is so wide the laser dings off his teeth as it flashes by.

Rave is twitching to the music in one corner, not quite on the actual dance floor, maybe half a shoe. His hair wangs about, slicing the air. In front of him a girl with nose piercings bends carefully from side to side to the music, like she's operating a loom. I can tell he doesn't fancy her because he's staring over her head towards the bar. I wouldn't say this was a bad night, per se. Just different.

I glance at the other tables. I smile at a girl with shiny lips, she smiles back. I look away. Ay-up Lee. I turn for a second look. She's still looking, but so's her boyfriend, not smiling. I turn away.

On the dance floor I can no longer see Raven. The pierced girl is still weaving away. Maybe he's in the Gents. Ned is dancing with a girl. He sways his body, throws his fringe out of his eyes. She is lovely, dark, delicate, twisting like seaweed. She watches Ned as she moves. Oh well. Good onya, knobhead. No point dwelling.

Lethal! It's Rave. His hair slices towards our table.

Look who I've got!

Behind him is Lorelle. She waves. My heart

148

explodes against my ribs. I sit up.

Well hello! I shout.

Hello, Lee! she calls.

She sits down at our table. She seems tiny, under-dressed. Her make-up glitters.

What would you like? yells Rave.

Watermelon Margarita please!

Rave is the night's unchallenged hero. This is his fifth sortie to the bar in unpredictable conditions and despite a shrinking cash fund.

How are you?

Fine! Yeah. You?

You look lovely!

Do you come here a lot?

Yeah! Yeah!

She sits back, takes it all in. She looks like she's been dipped in magic dust, even her hair. She fixes her glossy eyes on me.

Want to dance?

*   *   *

We are still kissing on the street at throwing-out time. We fall against walls, lamp posts. It is not possible to stop kissing, now we have started. She stands on her toes. She touches my jaw. She tastes like roses. From the corner of my eye I see Rave, his hair is nuked, it swings like a broken cable, and Ned, his arm around Raven's shoulder. Noddy and Big Ears. We stroll. Me and Lorelle learn to kiss as we go.

Come on! shouts Rave.

We stop near the all-night garage for Ned to be sick.

Shall we get a minicab? Lorelle says.

149

I don't tell her I can't afford it, that we're all cleaned out, brassic, less than.

OK you? I sign Ned.

Great! he signs back. Good days, Gog!

How long have you known sign language? Lorelle asks. Don't you speak Spanish as well?

Spanish, a bit of Italian, I say. I put my arm around her. I clear my throat.

Un poco, I say. Arrivederci. Buenos dias. Donde estan los bandoleros?

Woooooo! she says.

At the John Bell Business Park crossroads we go our separate ways. I offer to walk Lorelle home.

Sirrah! Lethal! Adieu, mate. See ya, Lorelle.

Rave and Ned womble off to the right while I take the left with the most stunning florist in the world.

What a beautiful night, I say. Look at the stars. The Big Dipper that is, by the way.

She takes off her shoes and tucks herself inside my jacket. This night is a night above all nights, a classic noche. I don't share this information with Lorelle. All good things come to those who wait.

We kiss in the shrubbery outside her house, we scuff up the path and kiss against her front door.

You have to go, she says. No funny business.

She lives with her mum.

No, no. Of course, I whisper. Flattening her against the door, pressing my thigh between hers.

Night, Lee.

Night. Night, then.

I back away down the path. I feel noble. I want to say something poetic. I can't think what.

Buonasera. I say. Buenos tardes. See you anon.

She disappears inside the house.

150

As I walk home I think, You nonce. See you anon? The only blot on an otherwise minted evening.

I can't sleep. I boil the kettle over and over. I have a shower at twenty past four a.m. I don't even know what anon means. Anonymous? Why would I see her anonymous? Knobbery. I wait till the sky lights up and then I send her a text:

Ther r butifl things in this world + ther is u. Lee.x U r 1drfl.

GENERALLY CLOUDY, DRIZZLE IN PLACES, TURNING
BRIGHT AND SUNNY LATE MORNING

I am cleared for landing. I am Lethal. She has texted me back.

> Hey u. c u for cofee? cafe nero? @ 1? dn't b L8! LX

Try to stop me.

A quick hair repair, a cold water emergency job, being that I am at work. At least I'm wearing my Lacostes.

I check myself in Tesco's window, not too bad. I don't need to make a big effort; she asked me, amigo. I see Crow sitting on a black bin outside Superdrug.

Tidings, Crow. Can't stop. Knob off, Birdbrain. I wave him away. He looks at me, glass-eyed, bounces twice and lifts off.

She has her back to the door. I consider putting my hands over her eyes but then I think, no.

Howdy. How goes?

Hi Lee. All right? Do you want a coffee?

Don't mind if I do. If the cappuccino's decent here. I shall just be a tickety tick tock. I join the back of the queue. She is prettier than ever. I am talking gibberish. Easy there, tiger.

I rejoin her. I try to resist an urge to rush—slow movements are the dance of seduction.

Nothing like real coffee beans I always say, I say.

She fixes me with her best seductive stare, full wattage. I am putty in her hands. Result.

Lee, she says. I just wanted to say. I just thought. You know. To let you know in fact that. The other night was great, don't get me wrong. But I wanted to tell you and be straight with you. Because I like you. I like you a lot. You are a good friend. I just don't think of you that way and the other night was a bit of a mistake, that's all. Do you know what I mean?

Lorelle raises her latte and sips. She rests it in the saucer and looks at me, froth on her lip.

Of course. No problem at all.

Yeah? Really? Sorry, Lee. I hope this is OK. I thought it probably would be. Are you OK?

Absolutely no problem whatsoever.

It's just I thought it best. Better than, you know? I thought we're such good friends and it would be such a shame.

I am in full and total agreement. No problem at all.

Thanks, Lee. I knew you'd be fine. Our friendship means a lot to me.

And me. And me. I totally get where you're coming from.

I think friendship is the most important thing, actually, she says.

So do I.

I'm so relieved, she says. You get mangled and next day you think, Oh my God. She laughs.

Just one of those things that occurs from time to time, I say. A natural occurrence, things occur. They occur.

Thanks, Lee. You're a star.

Zero problema. I'll get these.

I pay for our coffees. On the street she's pressed for time, as per.

Got to run. Nice to see you. Take care, Lee, yeah?

Yeah. You too. Mind how you go.

I walk for ages with an empty head. Nothing. Zero. Just one foot in front of. Then I think: Maybe she never fancied me, ever. Or maybe she did and went off me. Or possibly it was that night that did it. Or Ned. Ned throwing up at the garage. Maybe Ned put her off. Or I did, or we both did. Or maybe this whole thing has just been in my head all along. So near and yet so far. Lee Hart, you total knob. As if. What? Joking me. A girl like that. Time to get real, hombre. Snap out of it. Wake up and smell the.

I don't return to work. I walk home. My phone tings with messages from Derek. I don't answer. My legs take me. C'est la vie. C'est la vie. C'est la vie. End of.

*   *   *

Confidential is one of those words. It makes things formal. My letter to Colin Davenport at Greenacre Funeralcare Group PLC is *Confidential*. It says so on the envelope. I check the spelling so I don't come across as an arse. I only write one side so as not to detain him. I point out that, being on the young side, I am likely to be of good use to Greenacre, able to adapt and learn but also knowing, as I do, Shakespeare's establishment inside out. Knowing the ropes. I rattle on in the vernacular. Ready for duty. Ready to learn. Employee such as myself. A forward-thinking company like Greenacre. On I

154

rabbit. Hope you will consider me. Not just because. But also. Dedicated. What I have to offer. As well as. Looking forward to working for Greenacre. Joining the team. Yours sincerely. I read it through. I think, You're on, Lee Hart. I nearly hire myself.

*   *   *

Derek and me eat our sandwiches outside on the forecourt, between the hearses, in the sun, as if we're on holiday. Ham and pickle I've got. We are philosophical.

Derek says he wouldn't lower himself to Colin Davenport's level. Says he won't crawl for a job, not to anyone. I should not have begged, he says. I should have waited till they came to me, he says.

Derek does not live in the real world. Talk about cloud nine. It's dog eat dog these days.

Remember who taught you your trade, he says. Any cake?

I open the Mr Kipling Lemon Slices. Six in a pack for £1.40. Reasonable.

Derek gets wistful. In the heatwave of 2003 it was frontline action, he says. The elderly dropping like flies. No time to sleep or eat, he says. Full up at the inn. You have to say no, Health & Safety. When the chillers are full they're full, takes a few days to clear them. People are caught unawares.

Derek stares off up Seddlescombe Road, reliving it. The vulnerable can't survive extreme heat, he says. Ditto the cold snap of January 2004. Irene, he says, put fan heaters in the office to make a cosy corner for the living. Prepping clients, he says, his fingers were as stiff as the deceased's.

I'll miss the business, he says. Nothing else like it.

Hold your horses, I say. Not over yet.

It is for me, he says.

I have carried Colin Davenport's reply in my rucksack for a day and a half. Get it together, knobhead, I tell myself. Now or never. I pop to the only private place on the premises, hoping Derek doesn't notice my absence.

I lock the door, sit on the loo, tear open the envelope.

The word confidential does not feature in Colin Davenport's letter. As far as he's concerned I am free to wave it, along with my arse too, at the whole town and far beyond. Because he is very sorry but. He has nothing to offer at the present time, and while he realises this may come as something of a disappointment, he is confident I will find something in a related field soon. What with the current recession and cutbacks, these are belt-tightening times. Everyone is feeling the pinch, he says. Redundancies are always regrettable, but they have become necessary in today's climate. Difficult for everyone. A disappointment of course. Thank you for thinking of Greenacre. Wishing you all the best! And a rosy future in the trade. From all of us here.

Yours sincerely. Sincerely up yours.

Colin Davenport.

I open the pedal bin with my toe. Drop the letter in.

C'est la vie. Disappointing, but. No point dwelling. I feel tired. My head is heavy as. I lay it on the cistern. We will have to sell the cottage, pronto. No probs. Best thing. 'Tis the season. Old Frilly Ears said so.

27

PERHAPS A BRIGHT START BUT BECOMING CLOUDY,
WITH SHOWERY RAIN A LIKELIHOOD

There is no denying that spring has driven her sideshow into town. Buenos dias. These hedgerows are thick with insy flowers, birds zag, giant foxgloves stand at the side of the road. Game on. Even the sun has made an entrance and is lighting up the weather vanes and the church spire.

Things are supposed to change in the spring, nature knows it. I am the same old knob, but. A single event could change that any day soon. There is a certain je ne sais quoi in the air.

On the corner, just after the postbox, I stop. Have I come the wrong way? Mental or what? I look behind me. It is our lane. I look ahead. It is our cottage, but.

Words, spray-painted words, cover the brickwork, every inch. Blue and black words, taller than the windows, wide as the house, stretching and separating around corners, reaching up to the chimney. I stand a minute to read them. GOG IS AN ARSE. GOG IS NOT GOD. HELLO. GOG IS A KNOB. I AM A PRISONER. GOG IS A KNOB. GOG IS A KNOB.

This is him, always was. He will push push until. Everything I have done. All these years.

And this is how.

I run to the house.

Ned!

I jump the stairs two at a time, across the

landing, into his room. He is sitting on the windowsill, his back to me, his legs hanging out of the open window, gazing at the field. He doesn't hear me. He wouldn't. He doesn't turn.

I stare. He is blond. My dark-haired brother is. For a moment I don't know my own house, my own brother. Then the sound of a large penny dropping. Catch up, Lee. Wake up. Nordic stalker on the premises.

I bolt downstairs. After the chemo, before the naturopaths, she wore a short bleached wig when she lost her hair. Why not? she laughed, maybe I'll have more fun.

He must've found it, he must've discovered it in my room when I was at work.

I dive into the kitchen. Change of rules. Fine by me. I pick up the .22. I've done my best.

Come on then. I run back up. I am in charge of plans.

His room is empty this time, curtain blowing. Through the open window I see him running barefoot flat out along the set-aside towards the mast.

Ned!

I run. Two can play. I'll count you down. No probs.

I am at the mast before you can say Lee Hart is a knobhead, but.

Heavy sky, no wind. All I can hear is my breath and Crow rasping in the oaks. I go beyond the boundary into the woods. I wait, steady, listen. I could walk this path blind. No word of a lie. Not that I'm bragging, just saying. I am the trees and the wind and this ground. I am the bones of the woods. Every twitch I feel. No point him hiding, I'll

158

sniff him out. I am Lee. The woods'll give him up. Everything knows I'm here, everything that grows and crawls. I breathe in and the woods breathe out. Everything changes in the spring. I don't stop to think, there is nothing to think. I find him quick—I would. He stands looking at the canopies. Fascinated by the patterns, always was. He doesn't hear me—he wouldn't.

He will paralyse in a chair, like Lester. He will paralyse me first. He will end up, we will both end up, same old. Our family tradition, dead or dead as. Done with it, I am. Arrivederci. Very sorry, but.

I position myself, aim. His heart, his head. I could blind him at this distance. Oblivious, he is. Candy from a baby.

I hesitate. I breathe out. Come on.

He just stands there. For *fucks*.

I lower the weapon. I close my eyes. I can't. Call yourself a hunter?

I yell. Loud as. It sends the birds straight up from the trees. My ears buzz.

Ned gazes up at the birds. He raises his arms to them.

28

Becoming Warm in Sheltered Areas, Unsettled Later in the Evening, a Dry Night

I make mince and onion. Put a peeled onion in each room of your house you will never catch a cold, keep meaning to test that. Kitchen clock starts ticking again. I put the kettle on. I sit and rest my head on the table and fall asleep for maybe a minute.

I wake. The clock goes, Tick tock tick and then it forgets. I try to think. My mind is swinging about. Lee Hart, you have fucked up this time, it says. Talk about slow on the uptake. Might have known. No greater knobhead hath e'er. Whatever.

I shall have to report him to the police. They will want to question him. Best of luck with that. I don't know what he'll get. A warning? Community service? Detained at Her Majesty's? A police record. Nice one, Neds, that'll look good on your CV. Something to look forward to. *Good afternoon, Mr Hart. Please take a seat. Can you tell us when you first noticed your brother rambling the public bridleways in a ladies wig?*

I stand to do the dishes. I turn on the taps at the sink, drop the mugs into the foam. I stop to catch my breath. I look out at the field, the sky. I would like to tear it all down. Burn the field, burn the house. Let it all just. I feel my breath suck. Why does it? Why can't it fucking? I swing my fist through the window and listen to the glass shatter into tinkling pieces onto the path on the other side.

I lie on my bed. I have no idea what time it is but there is a rod of sunlight on the floor. My hand throbs. It is wrapped in something and taped over. I see him hovering, checking, closing the door, opening it again; this is all new to Ned. He looks like he's been asked a question to which he does not know the answer.

He brings me a tray. Soup and a sandwich and Panadol. Clear as day I see I should've done this years ago, step aside; let him be. I don't like cucumber. I take it out of the sandwich. He watches me eat. I don't ask if he has eaten. I don't ask anything. He watches carefully, his chin low, his hair in his eyes. He tries to breathe through his nose rather than his mouth. He chews his nails. Tearful, he looks. He touches my face.

No cry, Gog, he signs.

I shall have to correct him there. He needs telling. I open my mouth. Nothing. A squeak at the back of my throat. I gasp, I try to swallow. Ned stares.

In my head the voice of reason has arrived. Buenos dias. I pay attention. *Good afternoon, Mr Hart. Can you tell us why you have chosen to lie malingering here, boo-hooing and scoffing sandwiches, while your colleagues are all hard at work?* Ned reaches out, takes my hand. I do nothing. I lie there like a dead man, like one of our own dearly departed, while he fusses, wipes, breathes. *Is it or is it not the case you allow your brother to slice cucumbers with unwashed hands and patrol the highways in a state of semi-undress?* Ned examines my fingers, holds them. He presses them against his face. *While all the time paid-up clients lie waiting, uncremated, on Seddlescombe Road? Do you have anything to say, Mr Hart. Mr Hart?*

I have nothing to say. I close my eyes.

Ned is gone. The room is dim, dusk outside. The field has turned mauve in the half-light. I get up. I find my jacket, my keys. Downstairs the clock ticks loudly. I let myself out.

I sit with her at the edge of the field till the light in the sky is a pale thin line. The birds are roosted, silent. I will head back soon. Getting cold. I will make a plan. I will call the police. Then I think, what for? What for? Then I do nothing at all. Then it is dark.

When I think back down the years, it's like we were all holding on. To what? Some thread. Some chance of. Like one day we'd dance with roses between our teeth, as if we were the lucky few in a jackpot life. Life is a lottery, they say. No good wishing you had someone else's ticket. We are holding on still. Because it could all change tomorrow, things do, I know that much. That time in the kitchen, she and me, just the light from the oven timer, a slow dance to no music, just the sound of our shoes shuffling, turning, turning, like time on a clock, counting ourselves down.

Farming is no life, she told us. She wanted our lives to light up under our feet, like the yellow brick road. The world is your oyster, she said. You had to believe, belief was everything. She believed, we believed. The circus had packed up and gone but we stood there still, clapping, believing. A roll of the dice. You hope for sixes, everyone does. Sixes are rare, that's all.

I hear him. Midnight by now, or thereabouts. He calls my name, over and over. Looking for me. An animal noise. I listen. I let it go on.

*　　　*　　　*

It will not be the same from now. Time to go our separate ways. I tell him this next morning in the kitchen before I leave for work. He sits perfectly still in his pants and watches me sign. He pours out his own Cheerios. A first.

A new beginning, I sign him. I thumbs-up. He thumbs-up back.

Gog, he signs.

What? I'm late.

He smiles. Nothing, he signs.

Cheers, Neds. Laters.

*　　　*　　　*

I go the short route home. It rained earlier but now the air is clear. The trees drip. We're having chicken kebabs tonight. We bought our own skewers many moons back, with barbecue parties in mind. Nice evening, summer on its way. Maybe we will sit in the garden. I'll wipe down the bench.

I have bought chocolate mini rolls. Talk about pushing the boat out. Only joking. What's done is done, I reckon. Turn our attention to the future. I will make enquiries about the removal of aerosol-spray graffiti. Perhaps we will paint the house. At any rate we'll sell the house, as per original plan. A flat near town. A job. I can re-train. I'm only twenty-five, not old. Never say never. Ned will find a job, there are jobs in town. Fresh start, leave the rest behind.

The lane glows in the evening sun. The hedge has started its sproutings. I spot a tall flower in the ditch.

I'm home! Stupid really. Just a habit. Most habits are harmless.

The chocolate mini rolls are in my hand when I go into his room—a bit of brandishment I have in mind. *Look what I got. Not telling. Don't be a knob. Three guesses.*

Ned has a bigger surprise. In this regard he has blown me through plate glass. Checkmated for all eternity. Like a horse, a calf—some slaughterhouse thing—he is strung from the ceiling fan, feet dangling. Mid-air. Long and loose, limp as a snap-necked bullock. The force of my entry floats him slightly left.

I do not move. I stare.

Lee the visited. Him the messenger, hovering, silently talking of everything.

I can see he is gone, anyone would. Hours, looks like.

Rewind. Re-enter. Do not move, maybe it will stop.

Ned? It comes out as a question. For a moment I forget he is deaf.

When I go downstairs it is almost dark. I put the chocolate mini rolls in the bin.

We lie on the floor. I am out of breath. I stop blowing into his mouth. Ligature's done its job, closed his throat.

He is a skinny fuck, but. Twenty minutes, more, to get him down. This stuff was not designed to

164

be cut. They should incorporate plastic washing line on space shuttles. Here is an item that will not deteriorate or detach under any conditions. Plastic washing lines will inherit the earth along with the cockroaches.

He is heavy on my legs, pinning me down. Here lies my brother, Ned Joseph Hart. Poor Ned. God Almighty, Ned. What did you think. Here is my baby brother. What now? What in the name of. What were you. For fucks. What.

What!

I yell in his ear.

WHAT!

My voice enters the walls, the bricks, the spaces between. This house with its unspoilt views.

WHAT! WHAT!

That's it, Lee. Cry like a baby. Look at this. What have you done? What you have done.

*   *   *

My name is Lee Hart.

Address is number four Cinders Lane, Lye Cross.

My brother has hanged himself.

Ned Joseph Hart.

Twenty-three.

He is.

I have given CPR at the scene. No, no respiratory function.

Not medical, no. I am the trainee at Shakespeare's Funeral Services Ltd on Seddlescombe Road.

OK. Thank you.

Typical that he should choose death. Claim the thing that is mine. Now it is his.

TO THE SOUTH AND EAST SPELLS OF FINE, DRY WEATHER. POSSIBILITY OF SHOWERS IN THE WEST

I try to organise my thoughts. They resist. Think think. I lie on my back on the kitchen floor. The voice returns. *We have a few questions for you, Mr Hart, regarding your deceased brother, recently of this parish, and his various propensities. May we come in?*

I stare at the mop bang marks. Someone will paint over them, Sanderson Ivory in eggshell. That doll's house: where did it go? None of us could remember. The little people inside. You loved it. Hours and hours you spent. Every time you closed the door they all fell down.

Are you aware, Mr Hart, that there is abusive language currently defacing the exterior of this property? When you say, per se, Mr Hart, do you mean never? Or sometimes?

We saw CPR done at Fensham Leisure Centre once, remember? They did a display in the foyer. Talk about unrealistic. Cracked us up, total laugh. Come to think, it is perhaps only useful if you are standing beside the victim at the moment of respiratory failure, otherwise.

Spectacular view Mr Hart. Call that a risotto? Why did you throw a perfectly good packet of Six Cadbury's Mini Rolls in the bin? Is that kettle on?

Poor old Lee, they'll say. Remember Lee Hart? All on his lonesome. Never the same. Stark staring. Mental old spook alone with his dead men. Better off. He'd have been better off. Call me a knob but

I'm no fool. *Do you or do you not speak Spanish, Mr Hart? Mr Hart?*

We had a game when we were kids, you had to copy exactly, mirrors. Agreed, I could be more imaginative at the present time, but. The washing line feels cool on my neck. I stand in the centre of the room. Crow is here. He turns his mirror eye.

Evening, Lee. In a hurry? Late for your own funeral?

I look at Ned. He lies on his back, arms out. Ready to run, same as. *Watch me, Gog!* Over the dual carriageway, arms like a bird. Over the fields quick as, faster than. Woods, field, sky. Wait for me then. Wait for me. Like a photograph we wait.

*   *   *

Down the road the dead are still sleeping. Who knows what they dream, who they remember, where they go. You could envy them their untroubled time, but. I am not ready. Blackbird calls here each morning early before you open your eyes. Trick is to hear Blackbird. Trick is to carry on in spite of. Harder than it looks. Trick is to live. Not as easy as it sounds. Dead men teach it best. Live. Hold on. A trick worth learning.

The birds are throwing loops over the field. The hawthorn is finishing, hedgerows are turning green and the trees on the ridge are coming into leaf. She loved this time of year. Me and Ned used to pick the flowers we found on the verges, in the woods, and she'd put them in jars. Lee is my soldier, she used to say.

I fold up the washing line. I go downstairs to wait for the ambulance to arrive.

EPILOGUE

I take the bus to the interview, as it is some ten or twelve miles away from my flat. I carry my shoes in a plastic bag, so that they are clean when I arrive. From the bus stop I walk up an unfamiliar hill, bordered by Scots pine trees. Busy road, plenty of heavy haulage vehicles, but I enjoy the exercise.

I have lost the weight, almost all of it. I think to myself if I do this walk every day I will be fit as a butcher's dog. Result.

I arrive. I see there is a decent-sized car park. White posts and black chains, smart. I find a spot to change my footwear. I lean against the wall. I catch the sound of a crow, somewhere in the trees. I do not give it a second thought. I don't want to be late. Needs must.

I ring the bell.

T. J. Cotts Funeral Services. A handsome sign, hand-painted looks like.

A woman answers the door.

Hello. Mr Hart? Come in. Did you find us all right?

I did. No problem whatsoever.

Do have a seat. Can I get you any tea, coffee? Do you take milk? Sugar? Mr Cotts won't keep you a moment.

Thank you, I say.

Is it cold out?

No, I say. It's dry and bright. Bit of a wind from the west, but. Sunny spells are forecast for this afternoon.

Oh, that's nice, she says.

Yes, I say. Spring is here.

About time, she says.

Better late than never, I agree.

I loosen my jacket, adjust my tie, sit back. Land this one and I will be sorted. Fingers crossed.

Funny, if I had not worked at J. Winton's these last months I might not have qualified for this interview, due to the embalming experience required for this post. I had never met an embalmer before starting at Winton's, never mind assisted one. Embalming is not for everybody, but. Don't knock it till you've tried it, as we in the trade like to say. Good to keep the spirits up—what with the stiff competition—embalmers enjoy a joke, same as. Saying that, I would not have met Ruth either. A twist of fate, as they say.

I have sweaty palms. Take it easy. Deep breaths. I have never interviewed for funeral director. First time for everything. In with a chance. The job calls for experience. I have experience. I have good references. I have a steady hand, level head, a sense of humour. As far as boxes go it's tick tick tick.

Reminds me, I check my watch. I'm early. I could have caught the later bus, but time doesn't belong to you in this game, it belongs to those whose time is up. There lies a conundrum. Life is topsy-turvy in the land of the dead.

If I get this one, touch wood, I will give Derek a bell down there by the seaside. Get him out of his retirement deckchair.

Del, Guess what? Go on. No. Try again.

Reckon he'd be well chuffed.

Remember who taught you everything you know, he'll say.

And I'll go, Er, wait. Tip of my tongue. Hang

172

about. No, it's gone.

I walked past Shakespeare's the other day. They've painted it. A new sign up: *Greenacre Funeral Services. Part of Greenacre Group Plc.* Below that it says: *Professional. Discreet. The people you can turn to.* I didn't stop or glance in. I just kept going.

The sun flashes patterns through the window, strobing the walls. Similar pale wallpaper to Shakespeare's, as I recall.

I think of Ned. I close my eyes. Knobster. There he is, mid-sky, mid-twang. Arms wide, frog legs, head back. A photograph.

Gog! Why can't it always be like this?

I see us, me and him. Towards the mast we stroll, same as. To the woods where the air is green, along the paths where the tree roots grow. A laugh, seriously mental underfoot. These beech are two hundred years old. Buenos dias. They weave like webs. I watch him gawping up at the canopies— higher than high—mouth open, hands talking, beads raining, as per. Gog! Watch me.

I do watch him, I always did: daring cars to hit, the sky to fall, the world to open, like the oyster he was promised.

We are running, me and Ned. Same old, same as. A long way, a million miles. Lanes, fields, woods. Giddy up. Our carriage is invisible. It flies quicker than the wind, than the speeding sky. No one sees us. Adios. We are galloping galloping gone.

ACKNOWLEDGEMENTS

My grateful thanks to the staff at the funeral home in the south-east of England, who generously allowed me to regularly intrude upon and observe their work at close quarters, and who patiently endured all my questions.

My thanks also to my agent, Clare Alexander, to Dan Franklin, Steven Messer, Suzanne Dean and all at Cape. And to Philip Davis, Esther Freud, Victoria Jenkins, Marylou Soto, and Robyn Becker. My love and thanks to Mark.

Thank you to Pam and Yi at the deaf and sign language social enterprise, Femaura, in London.